The Wizdom
of Oz

Philippa Merivale

BOOKS

Winchester, UK
Washington, USA

The Wizdom
of Oz

First published by O Books, 2010
O Books is an imprint of John Hunt Publishing Ltd., The Bothy, Deershot Lodge, Park Lane, Ropley,
Hants, SO24 0BE, UK
office1@o-books.net
www.o-books.net

Distribution in:

UK and Europe
Orca Book Services
orders@orcabookservices.co.uk
Tel: 01202 665432 Fax: 01202 666219
Int. code (44)

USA and Canada
NBN
custserv@nbnbooks.com
Tel: 1 800 462 6420 Fax: 1 800 338 4550

Australia and New Zealand
Brumby Books
sales@brumbybooks.com.au
Tel: 61 3 9761 5535 Fax: 61 3 9761 7095

Far East (offices in Singapore, Thailand,
Hong Kong, Taiwan)
Pansing Distribution Pte Ltd
kemal@pansing.com
Tel: 65 6319 9939 Fax: 65 6462 5761

South Africa
Stephan Phillips (pty) Ltd
Email: orders@stephanphillips.com
Tel: 27 21 4489839 Telefax: 27 21 4479879

Text copyright Philippa Merivale 2009

Design: Stuart Davies

ISBN: 978 1 84694 318 8

A CIP catalogue record for this book is available
from the British Library.

Printed by Digital Book Print

O Books operates a distinctive and ethical publishing philosophy in
all areas of its business, from its global network of authors to
production and worldwide distribution.

CONTENTS

This book is dedicated to Nicola, Stephen and Magdalen.
I love you all with all my heart.

Introduction

L. Frank Baum's colorful creation caught my attention some years ago and has continued to intrigue me. His narrative made useful fodder for workshops – color and light is an excellent tool for encouraging personal empowerment – but I knew there was something else to be done with his witches and wizards: it was not for nothing that novelists and polemicists such as Gore Vidal, Salman Rushdie and others had long engaged with Oz as a source of more than mild fantasy.

When I put the idea of this short book to John Hunt, publisher of O Books and ex-editor from heaven (or Oz), he responded at once in the affirmative, adding that it needed framing. After this clear pointer and a brief conversation with John, it was only a short time before Theo – the ageing Professor who introduces himself overleaf – showed up and quite swiftly melded in my mind not only with the illustrious Wizard but with the figure of Baum himself, whom I have long suspected to have been consciously doing rather more in his books than he claimed when he wrote in 1900, 'The Wonderful Wizard of Oz was written solely to please children of today.' Baum and his wife were members of the Theosophical Society, whose stated aims are to explore the hidden laws of nature and the unexplored latent powers in man. I knew little else about this author, except that before embarking in middle age on the children's fiction for which he became so renowned, he had tried and failed at a number of ways to support his family. I had also heard that he lived in Chicago.

I'm fond of California so when it felt necessary to place Theo and his friends in a geographical location, I randomly chose San Diego, which I have never seen but should like to. So it was a happy little moment when a friend and colleague happened to remark, a few weeks later when the first draft of this book was complete, that Baum is believed to have written *The Wizard of Oz* while on holiday in Coronado Island, San Diego. I have a suspicion that Theo, at the very least, would agree with me when I say that nothing happens by chance.

Dorothy, the timeless young heroine of Oz, represents of course everywoman, everyman: she has adapted herself for well over a century to fit a multitude of cultures, stages and interpretations. You can revisit Oz through this re-presentation of the story in less than a couple of hours, but I hope that as you do so, a light bulb may flash in your heart and soul, which will help to light your own way 'home' – to the often-hidden place within you where the seeds of your happiness and fulfillment lie, patiently waiting to be watered and sparked into life.

Meanwhile, enjoy the story: it's not only timeless but full of delights.

P. M.

The Professor

'They say you go through life but they're wrong, you know. It's life that goes through *you*.'

This was Theo, the old Professor. He should have retired years ago but he loved his work too much. End of every term he said goodbye; start of next session he magically reappeared with something new to teach. Usually something a little quirky.

'Think about it,' he said. 'There's really nothing static or solid about very much of our experience; life isn't a series of railroad stations, places you get to one after another, nicely fixed in firm locations. The thing we call life is fluid, a stream of energy, dynamic. Its flow moves through you and you can do what you like with it: it's yours to bend and shape. You're artists, you see.'

They were in the bar where they often went after their Friday lectures, sometimes spending an hour or two with the man who had been teacher to all of them at one time or another. Greg called him Grandpa

Heidi didn't feel like an artist, not at all. They were coming up to their last term in college: there were finals to face and then... Frank and Yasmin had careers fixed already, the others were catching up fast, but Heidi didn't feel so sure.

'So you mean it's pretty much like they say it is: the only thing you can be sure about is everything will change,' she said. 'Makes me feel a bit seasick.'

'Except sometimes – like when you want it to change,' the Professor replied.

Joseph looked hopeful – just slightly – for the first time in a while.

'They come fast or slow, the changes,' Theo went on. 'But they come anyway.'

'Like you're calmly going along doing your thing and then a sudden phone call changes your life,' said Heidi.

'Sometimes,' said Theo, 'but it doesn't have to be dramatic. Try throwing the same party twice or asking a tree to hold its blossom: not a hope.'

'Which means that bad things don't stay bad either,' said Yasmin.

'Exactly,' agreed Theo. 'Move with the wave and you'll find yourself just where you need to be. What was your favorite story when you were young?' he asked suddenly. 'Any of you.' He had a habit of throwing in questions or comments that seemed to come from nowhere in particular.

'I adored Narnia,' said Greg. 'I lived there for years.'

'Aladdin!' said Yasmin. 'The flying carpet was my dream.'

'I loved the one about a spider,' said Dawn. 'He saved the animals' lives somehow by weaving messages for them into his web. Don't remember the details – it made me cry but I still went back for more.'

'Great stories,' Theo replied. 'You could write a thesis on any of them.'

'I guess that's what my dad meant, in a way,' said Heidi, 'when he used to tell me the best children's stories were written for grown-ups. Or for grown-ups too, anyway.'

'Your dad was a wise fellow,' said Theo. 'What was your favorite story, Heidi?'

'*The Wizard of Oz*,' she replied. 'Way top of my hit parade.'

'Funny, that,' said the old man. 'It's always been my favorite, too.'

'I never read the book,' said Joseph. 'My kid sister watched the movie over and over. There was an awful lot of paint.'

'Yummy,' said Dawn. 'All those bright colors – I loved them. It was my best, best thing for a while; came around every Christmas. I was convinced I was Judy Garland, of course; asked Santa for ruby slippers. Well, red shoes.'

'I wonder why I'm not surprised by that.' Theo's eyes twinkled as he looked at Dawn over his half-moon glasses. Dawn looked at him quizzically.

'You always seem to know more about us than we know about ourselves,' said Frank. 'It's quite disconcerting. Or maybe it's reassuring...'

'Oh but I don't know more about you,' said Theo. 'No-one will ever know you better than you know yourselves. As Oz himself, you might find, would be the judge.'

'My mom always wondered why the Oz movie never bored her like you'd think it would,' said Yasmin. 'She said Glinda – you know that pink, flouncy, goody-goody Witch – reminded her of me. Not a compliment. I far preferred the wicked black one – oh and the flying monkeys, of course.'

'I don't see Glinda bungee-jumping,' agreed Heidi. Yasmin was a lithe, bronzed athlete; she loved nothing more than clambering up a cliff edge or surfing a mountain-sized wave: not an obvious match for a fairy in frills.

'My dad used to read all the Oz books to me when I was little,' Heidi went on, 'and he loved to sit down with me and watch the movie. When I was older he said we all live in Kansas and we're all trying to get over there ourselves, to that brightly-colored planet. I was seventeen when he died but I still felt sometimes it was Oz he'd flown off to...'

'Maybe it was,' said Theo, 'in a way. And he was right, you know, we're all trying to find something, reach somewhere.'

'The movie goes back a few generations,' said Greg. 'The story's even older; but it keeps returning: new versions, new takes. It's stood the test of time, I guess. D'you think its images are still relevant to us now?'

'Pretty relevant,' Theo replied. 'Human nature doesn't change too fast. You've probably noticed that the so-called Wizard acts like an old duffer but behind the bluster he sees plenty more than he pretends. The man who wrote the story was a bit wizened when he did it – well, forty-something at least – been bankrupt a time or two; tried his hand as a reporter, a road salesman – no takers. Then he decided on kids' books and before long, *whizz* – shot to fame. When you've been around a while, you know a thing or two. Bit of a wizard himself, I shouldn't wonder.'

'Do I get your drift?' Heidi asked. 'D'you think as an author he might even have been with you on that thing you said just now, about life being an energy stream, the source or resource we're given to make things with?'

'Maybe even that,' Theo replied. 'Who knows what magic the Emerald City held for him? Or the Yellow Brick Road that led there.'

'I'll tell you one thing,' Heidi continued. 'I get that Dawn's an artist of sorts; and Greg is; and all of you are. If *I'm* supposed to be an artist of some kind – any kind – I sure as heck haven't a clue how I'm meant to be getting there. I can't draw, I can't sing.'

'You can't win writing contests,' said Theo.

'Oh that,' she poofed. 'It was a small one. The competition was pretty tame.'

'And you did it. But here's the thing…' their teacher continued, 'We script our lives, or we sculpt them – with our beliefs, our thoughts, the way we influence that wonderful stream of life that flows through us. You're creating your own stories – your life experiences – all the time, through the energy that's carried in your thoughts.'

'*Whoa*…' said Yasmin. 'How likely is that?'

'On a scale of one to ten?' The teacher's dark eyes twinkled again. 'I'd give it a high nine, higher. You just don't notice the thoughts that you're quietly pouring into your life-stream while you're busy doing something else. Everything that has ever happened in the world started out as a thought. It may be an idea about inventing a way of getting around, starting a new business, or getting rich in some way or other; it may be an urge to have a baby, design an engine.'

'Or a building,' said Joseph. He was the architect with the passionate ideas – when his passions weren't quenched by temporary blips of the heart.

'A building, yes; a play, a song. It may be something less ambitious: the thought to spend some extra time with an ageing relative; the thought to make a new friend or look after the one we've already got.'

'That's an art,' said Frank.

'Of the most useful kind,' agreed Theo. 'Or there's the thought to be patient,' he continued, 'or independent. Or write a song, bake a cake. And the Wizard knows it. He knows the power of thought. That's why he pushes that most endearing central character, Dorothy the adventurer, to sort things out for herself – through the power of her thoughts, or her active dreaming.'

'We never learned that in school,' commented Greg.

'Perhaps it's time for a change of curriculum,' suggested Theo.' You know what? You'll all be setting off on your own paths through life before long. Sometimes that feels exciting, sometimes it's scary. You'll run up against road blocks of one sort or another, things get in your way. Stuff happens, in other words – usually when you think you've planned something else entirely. Some power, the personal kind, will come in handy.'

'When I was a kid,' Frank remarked, 'I thought that being grown up was a kind of magic state of being you reached, a sort of line you stepped over; after you got there you would be able to handle them all – those road blocks as you call them – whatever they were. You know: people might be jobless and penniless, one-legged and ninety-eight years old – whatever – but they were adults so it must be OK. I think I vaguely believed something like that powerful, managing adult thing would happen when you got to be twenty-something. Now I'm pretty much there and it doesn't look so simple.'

The Professor gazed for a moment at the young business scientist who picked up merit awards standing on his head.

'No,' agreed the Professor, 'it's never simple – but always interesting. And for the most part it's exactly the blocks or the difficulties that make it interesting. They come in all shapes and sizes, you know, those obstacles.'

'Like?' asked Yasmin. She tended to sail through life oblivious to obstacles.

'Like?' Theo replied. 'Let's see now. Watching that gold trophy slip out of your sight, for instance? The agony as the silver one was handed to you on the rostrum?'

'Oh yes,' she groaned. 'That was probably the worst thing that ever happened...'

'My heart bleeds,' laughed Theo. 'Of course, there are one or two other things in life that might occasionally be problematic – even for you.'

'I believe you,' said Yasmin. 'I really do. *Er...* what kinds of things?'

'All sorts,' Theo replied. 'Partner half-hears you. Boss half-sees you. Mother-in-law grumbles at you. Kids act like you don't exist. Business crumbles around your ears. OK, so not much of that has happened for you yet – and just as well. But maybe a parent or a friend has turned deaf a time or two – with the best will in the world, of course. Or, let me see now...'

'Lover teams up with a baseball player,' Joseph interrupted lugubriously.

'I know, I know,' sighed Theo.

'Best mate leaves town,' added Dawn.

'Dad disowns you,' said Greg. 'More or less.'

'All of that,' said the teacher. 'Or maybe none of it; perhaps more nebulous stuff instead. You're not too sure where you're going, or why – or even how you landed where you are. Mild, free-floating anxiety, perhaps, frustration, boredom, energy below par; life up for some kind of renewal, if only you knew what kind that might be; an unformed but nagging conviction that *there must be more to life than this*.'

'Feels kind of familiar,' said Frank.

'Well there *is*; there's plenty more to life than this!' Theo continued cheerfully. 'Trust me – or rather, trust Dorothy, that champion of Oz. She'd know exactly how you feel. She would take any of the above irritations or deprivations, and rack them up a few notches.'

'And then color them grey,' suggested Heidi.

'Exactly,' said the Professor. 'And if you want in-your-face, fully frustrating, dull – the kind you can't miss if you try – then check out those Kansas prairies of hers. No mom and dad, no toys, no love, no school, no playmates, no fruit, flowers, grass; only kindly but drab companions and a horrible neighbor. It's so downbeat, even the color got up and left.'

'Well, *there's* a sad beginning to a story,' said Joseph.

'And generation after generation has loved it,' commented Greg.

'So the Wiz believes we write our own outcomes,' said Dawn. 'Or you believe we do, anyway. I promise you I can think of a few endings I didn't write. Or the writing got pretty scrambled in that life-stream you were telling us about.'

'We can all find plenty of scrambled outcomes,' replied Theo. 'Or strangled ones. We break bones, or the only job we've ever wanted goes to someone else. But the Wizard may have a different explanation for how those outcomes come about.'

'Does he have some suggestions?' suggested Frank. 'Does he offer ways to dream up better endings?'

'He has some shrewd ideas about avoiding the worst of the road blocks, or dissolving them when you run up against them. And about how to be creative – in the way you want to be, so your life becomes a script you actually meant to write, not the one that just happened to you by accident. He even throws in brightly colored signals here and there – like clues on a treasure hunt.'

Heidi's eyes lit up. This was ringing a few bells about things her father had pointed out to her in those ancient days exploring Oz.

'Here's an idea,' said Theo. 'How about we look at this little parable rather more closely? How about a module – extra-curricular, I need hardly say? My little gift to you before you start running up against your own special road blocks, and dissolving them, of course, which is where the fun begins. We could call it "The Wizdom of Oz".'

'Cool!' said Heidi. 'I'd love that!'

'I'm up for that too,' agreed Frank. 'I don't know the story but I do know *you*.'

'I must admit...' said Joseph, hesitating a little, 'it could maybe...'

'Be fun,' suggested Dawn.

'And each time we consult the Wiz,' said the Professor, 'we'll look at some of his recipes for dreaming up a world of your choice, and starting to make it happen. Sound good?'

'Sounds like exactly what I need,' said Greg.

'When can we start?' asked Yasmin.

The old man looked at his watch.

'In about three hours' time?' he said.

Be Careful What You Wish For

The Professor lived in a forested area outside town: mountains rose into the distance behind the house; on a good day you could see the ocean stretching ahead of it. The timber-built home was a shabby relic of an earlier age. Frank would have liked to give the doors and windows a fresh coat of paint. Heidi thought it was the friendliest place she'd ever seen.

It was early evening; the last rays of late-winter sunshine beamed through a slightly open window as the group settled down in their teacher's favorite room. Generations of students had sat around this battered kitchen table, its surface a mosaic of stains: tea, wine, ink, the grateful marks of history.

'Never, *ever*, sell out on your dreams,' the old man said.

'We don't need to sell out on our dreams,' replied Joseph, more than a little sulkily. 'Other people will obligingly do that for us. Don't even have to *ask* them.'

'Is that so? Is that really so?' Theo looked at Joseph: one of those gentle, penetrating laser-beam looks that traveled like fluid light through the pupils of the young man's eyes and landed somewhere in his entrails. Faintly uncomfortable, Joseph shifted in his seat.

'Never, *ever*, sell out on your dreams,' Theo repeated, setting down a large pot of steaming coffee. 'They are the imprint of your soul. You can harness the power of the winds and the sun, but first you need the dream. Dreams are the blueprint for all of your inventions, from a half-voltage love affair to a trip through space.'

'I can't even imagine a *half*-voltage love affair,' said Joseph. "Wish I could," he added tetchily.

'Better picture a flying trip instead,' said Yasmin, the eternal explorer. 'Bet you can conjure that up if you try.'

'Just like Dorothy did,' said Heidi. 'She *really* needed a

dream.'

'She sure did,' agreed Theo. 'And so do you.'

Heidi's grades were good, not great. Her specialty had more to do with looking out for her friends and loved ones and less to do with stacking up credentials. Ask her why she was studying psychology and she'd say she liked people-watching, which was true in more ways than one. But Heidi's ways of people-watching didn't tick the boxes she thought she might be needing in the next few years. She would soon have to start carving out a path of her own through life and she knew it.

'Why don't you remind us how the story runs?' Theo suggested.

'It's your class!' she exclaimed.

'Chapter One, please,' he replied. 'We need an expert to start us off.'

'Er...' Heidi hesitated a little. 'All right, then. There's this kid called Dorothy and she's living a bum life in the middle of nowhere. Everything's grey and lifeless – it's called the Kansas prairies in the story. Nothing seems to grow there, the trees are kind of bare and deadish-looking. The pigs are just about the only livestock – well, they can eat more or less anything that no-one else wants, can't they? Oh and Dorothy's an orphan, she lives with some dreary relatives. There's an uncle, Uncle...'

'Henry,' said Dawn.

'That's right. He works 24/7 and never opens his mouth – except to eat from time to time, I guess. Never a word, never a joke or a hug. And the aunt, Aunt Em, she screams if Dorothy dares to smile – well, laugh. So Dorothy doesn't get to chat a lot.'

'It's not so bad,' commented Yasmin. 'For an afternoon social she can always go down the yard, hang out with the sows. They're friendly enough.'

'Or walk the dog,' agreed Dawn.

'Who's called Toto,' said Heidi. 'And even that's not so easy. There's that vile woman next door. She hates Dorothy, hates the dog. Remember how she steals Toto and says she'll bump him off?'

'Where exactly is she, I wonder, that dear child?' mused the Professor, dreamily. 'Do you suppose she's about to start enjoying a beautiful reverie, as she slumbers deep?'

'No way!' exclaimed Heidi. 'Oz is a real place, I insist on it – far more real than those dreary Kansas prairies. She's on her way there right now: she just has to find it – this land she's been thinking about.'

'Ah,' said Theo, 'and therein lies the test, brave child. How convenient that a rainbow is called to her aid! Nevertheless, just suppose for a moment that this adventure of hers *were* a dream, then everything around her would be a symbol, would it not? Much like life itself: we're dreaming anyway, if we only knew it. There are so many little messages that come flashing up from the hidden stash of wisdom inside us, it's hard to stop the flow.'

'Toto's a good symbol, then,' said Dawn. 'Certainly a constant one – he never goes away.'

'A dog is the most faithful creature on the planet,' said Greg. 'And hey, the word looks like "God" spelt backwards. I never noticed that before.'

'Good thought,' agreed Theo. 'I'd say Toto is Dorothy's totem – of faith, of truth, steadfast as you like. He's Dorothy's reminder that she'll be faithful to herself no matter what. And there may be quite a lot of "what". You know the kind of thing,' he went on, looking at Greg. 'You really need that bursary to do the next year's study: it goes to someone else; you do the year anyway. Or,' he added, glancing at Heidi, 'you care 100 percent what your mom's going through, but you can't do it for her, you can't save her from herself – especially by sacrificing *your* self.'

'Too right,' said Greg.

'Dorothy really does have it tough, though,' said Dawn. 'I mean, she's lost more or less everything any of us might have ever wanted before the story's even begun. Love, companionship, basic security – the lot.'

'Color, even,' said Heidi. 'Imagine waking up every morning and finding the whole world's steeped in grey.'

'You know what?' said the Professor. 'An awful lot of journeys start that way. You lose everything – or at least you lose the thing you thought you wanted the most. Your whole world turns to a drab shade of nothing. So you start looking to find it again, whatever the "it" is that's been lost. And that's where the journey has a habit of getting interesting. Or even when we lose just one thing – a job, let's say...'

'Or a partner,' suggested Yasmin, pushing some chocolate biscuits towards Joseph.

'Or your parents' sanity,' added Heidi, with a feisty look at Greg.

'Then the search is on,' continued Theo. 'Yes?'

'Yep,' Greg agreed. 'The search is on, and it does get interesting, by the way.'

'Let me know when it starts, OK,' said Joseph. 'The interesting bit!'

'Oh you'll find that out soon enough,' said Theo. 'So what does this kid, this plucky young adventurer, do when the neighbor's shenanigans get to be all too much? The woman is the arch-persecutor, after all. And even the kindly farm laborers don't have more than a minute or two to console Dorothy. What does she do?'

'She dreams!' said Yasmin.

'A dream within a dream,' suggested Frank.

'Maybe,' agreed the Professor. 'Maybe she's dreaming actively, or consciously, which is what we all need to do as a regular thing: using the power of our active thought, to dream up the optimum scene. The outside may look all dark and grey – her inner world has felt pretty monochromatic too, come to that – but perhaps she's starting to dig right down, or expand right out. She's looking for light, after a fashion. Rather like any of us do when we're up against a problem: we try to throw some light on it.'

'There's been a power cut!' said Heidi. 'Kansas has been hit by a power cut; and that's before the storm even *begins*.'

'That's just what's going on,' said Theo. 'A cut in personal power. There's been a total eclipse of the sun – or a total eclipse of the heart, it's much the same thing.'

'So if they need to turn the power back on,' said Heidi, 'then maybe Dorothy's going to be the one to do it for them. My dad always told me if I want someone to change I just have to change myself – bingo! Easily said, of course – but look at Dorothy's plight, in the middle of that massive power failure. She's got an awful lot of work to do.'

'It's just a test,' said Theo. 'And what's the first thing we do when we think we've got no power – or resources of any kind, for that matter?'

He looked around at the group of friends, their usually expectant faces slightly blank.

'What do we do,' he repeated, 'when it feels like we've got no happiness or talent or success? Or wealth, come to that, or beauty, or anything you like.'

'Get depressed?' suggested Frank.

'That's quite possible,' conceded the Professor. 'But we look to other people to solve the problem, that's the point: we say she's prettier, he's richer, they've got better jobs – I want it. We forget they're all there inside us, all the resources we could ever need, so we try to grab them from outside.'

'That's true!' exclaimed Dawn suddenly. 'I think I've done that – or thought it – loads of times. Someone, anyone, give me what I haven't got!'

'Or else I'll take it from you anyway!' said Theo. 'Your time, your sympathy, your cash, your love – even your fear's better than nothing. That's why the bad-tempered neighbor bullies Dorothy, just to get herself some power – some energy, if you like, or some life-force – but she can only do that because

Dorothy's not remembered who she is. Not yet.'

'But she's starting to remember,' said Yasmin. 'You know that song she sings in the movie? It's all about a place she kind of dimly remembers, a place that's somewhere over the rainbow – that great new earth that she heard of "once in a lullaby".'

'Before she got to be an orphan,' said Heidi.

'Exactly,' agreed Theo, 'while she was still in touch with all that primeval power, soul-power, even – you could say the other side of the rainbow represented that distant time in her memory, before she was even born; before she left home, in a way.'

'I heard about these parents the other day,' said Dawn. 'They'd just had a new baby and the older child wanted to be alone with her. They were worried she'd be jealous, but they finished up putting the little girl in the baby's room and listening at the door. The child was whispering to her new sister, "What's God like? I'm beginning to forget."'

'"Out of the mouths of babes…"' said the Professor. 'We have a lot to learn from small children. They're clearer than we are, on the whole. They've not yet forgotten who they are. Maybe that's why we're following Dorothy's travels.'

'And maybe Dorothy's starting to un-forget!' said Heidi.

'She's turning the beam up,' said the Professor. 'Turning the lights back on. With a higher charge, she can make her dreams work for her. It's quite a vision she's creating, what with happy little bluebirds and skies and rainbows and all the rest of it. She's really feeling it, properly believing that she can make her dreams real.'

'Hey, Jo,' said Greg, 'maybe desperation can be useful? Maybe sometimes it's exactly what's needed to push you into a different gear. We can get buried or drowned – or get creative. Like you said, we can think up some grand designs.'

Joseph looked up, a glimmer lighting up his eyes and mouth.

'And then,' added Theo, 'you find that the worst thing that could ever happen sometimes turns into the best. Because look at something for a moment, Jo: look at the time – all of that year and a half, or whatever it was – *before* Kate finally took off with that baseball player. What would you say was the thought that you had most often – about the thing you had going with her?'

Joseph looked awkward as he turned his face towards the floor.

'You don't need to think too long about it,' said his teacher gently. 'All you need is a word – the first one that comes to mind.'

'*Er...* fear,' said Joseph. 'Worry,' he added. 'Stress, angst, confusion! Throw in a handful of jealousy and resentment...'

'Exactly,' agreed the Professor. 'That was the hidden agenda. Rather more Kansas-like than you might have cared to admit at the time. All those cumbersome emotions, shutting down the heart: probably not expressed too often, but sitting there like a shadow underneath everything else. Not really the most comfortable traveling companions, were they?'

'No,' conceded Joseph. 'It kind of made me nervous, all of it. If they'd ever made lilies in coffee-and-ebony, for heaven's sake, they would have looked like Kate. Walk around with a vision like that, you're bombarded – and it's not you they want to talk to. Made me shaky. Not to say invisible.'

'You still did fantastic work through all of it,' said Dawn. 'But it showed. You were stressed out with the whole thing. You even said she was all spin and no content.'

'Wrong,' said Heidi. 'It's not true of anyone, that.'

'Well, she *is* a dancer...' commented Joseph, a rueful grin spreading across his face.

'I know it's not true,' said Dawn. 'But the fact you even said it showed how you were feeling. And it's a totally normal state, that "I'm not good enough". Look at Paul Newman: kept thinking he was no good at his job, that he'd get found out! Look at me: I desperately wanted the place at Yale. There was nothing more important than being as good as my big sister. I was terrified I wasn't going to make it – you should have seen me at the interview. It was terrible.'

'So you finished up here with all of us!' said Yasmin cheerily. 'In the funnest city on earth. Best thing that could ever happen to anyone.'

'It was, in fact,' agreed Dawn. 'If I'd got the place I wanted, I'd probably have spent three years worrying about keeping up with my sister's awesome reputation. Not getting it set me free. But I was actually *unhappy* about coming to California – you remember?'

'And being as bright as they come, you created that so-called failure how, exactly?' asked the Professor. 'What was your dominating belief about yourself?'

'Dunce,' replied Dawn. 'Not enough, in any way you like to put a name on.'

'That was easy!' chuckled Theo. 'Like Dorothy. And like quite a few people in this room who could echo that. *Huh?*'

Heidi stuck a hand up. Joseph followed.

'And you've had a pretty good time of it anyway,' Theo continued, 'so let's not be too fearsome about fear. Just mindful: mindful that if you can dream up some pretty OK situations from a fear-base, a place where you don't even notice the thoughts that you're thinking, just imagine what you can do when you turn up the beam and start noticing. Because your underlying thoughts and beliefs – and they're mostly well unconscious, by the way – are really your wishes, in the sense of "make a wish".

'*One day I'll wish upon a star,*' sang Heidi, drumming gently on the table with her fingers.

'And sooner than you think,' said Theo. 'So here's the thing, here's our Friday agenda, or part of it: you're going to start making your wishes just a bit more conscious, a bit more aware. It's called connecting with your power.'

'Or lighting up the Kansas prairies!' said Greg, with a broad grin.

'Exactly,' agreed the Professor.

'Dorothy's still walking around in her fear-base, though,' commented Heidi. 'She's sung that great song and everything, but life is still quite bad. That's why she's about to go off and look for help. She wants to find herself a Wizard; she wants someone who will cancel out all her problems.'

'So would I, if my neighbor threatened to murder my dog,' said Dawn. 'Any gypsy in a vintage caravan would be better than that hideous crone next door.'

'Much under-rated and under-valued.' Yasmin leapt to the defense of the crone. 'The story would be lethally boring without her.'

'You're always up for a dose of adrenaline,' said Joseph. 'You've got a point, though.'

'Nothing like a good villain,' agreed Theo. 'And the same is true in life, of course. Vital catalyst, the villain. So yes, our heroine is looking for a Wizard. It's her first step in making conscious wishes. She finds him, after a fashion. It may look like a gypsy caravan the old man is living in, but this fellow she's run up against is no less a person than Professor Marvel himself. Who gives her, if I remember rightly, a valuable piece of advice: he urges her to find her way home.'

'Before the storm hits,' said Heidi.

'And before she finds that all that wishing she's just been doing has been rather more effective than she might have imagined. Because she's hardly back in that hovel of a house she lives in than it's whipped up from the drab piece of turf and hurled through the sky. It seems to be heading for the rainbow – and fast.'

'With Toto on board,' said Dawn.

'And just as well. So here's the Wizard's first lesson: look at exactly what it is you've been wishing for. What are you thinking about, ongoingly? What's the tone, the background hum, that underlies your typical stream of thoughts as you leave for class in the morning, eat lunch, take a shower? What are you hoping for? What have you *already* been thinking about, wishing and hoping for? Or thinking about and dreading – because either way you're energizing it. And where did those rather vague, absent-minded musings get you?'

'Not too far,' replied Heidi at once.

'I wouldn't be so certain,' continued the Professor. 'They probably took you to the perfect place – our worst-laid plans tend to throw up wonderfully useful lessons and many of our medium-laid plans are perfectly adequate. For the time being,' he added. 'Nevertheless, they can always get *better*. In a world of infinite choice, you might decide to tweak your landings, or endings, a little – more trophies and fewer wooden spoons, so to say.'

'That's quite some assignment,' said Heidi cheerfully, 'given out by the Wizard that we've not even met yet!'

'Ah, but he's there,' said Theo, 'right from the very beginning. Certainly from the moment Dorothy runs into Professor Marvel. Actually he's been there far longer than that – it's just that Dorothy doesn't know it yet.'

'Really?' said Heidi. 'I'd never noticed him there before…'

'Well, you'll start meeting him shortly,' her teacher replied. 'He begins to show up when we start looking for him. I'll see you next week. And remember those wishes of yours. Have a good look at them; check them out. Find out if you're quite sure that they're going to bring you the thing that you *really* want.'

The Oracle

When they climbed the rambling steps to the Professor's front door a week later, a notice was pinned over the top of it.

'Know Thyself,' it read.

'I'm working on it,' said Heidi.

'Am I worth knowing?' chuckled Dawn.

'Give me half a chance to find out,' said Frank, 'and I'll tell you. *Come into the garden, Maud,*' he warbled, '*I'll be there at the gates alone.* How about Sunday?' he added, reaching for her thick red ponytail.

'I'm busy, thanks,' Dawn replied, dodging.

'I don't know why you two don't just get on with it,' said Yasmin.

'Oh my goodness,' said the Professor, feigning surprise as he opened the door. 'How time does fly. Is it really Friday already? Come on in.'

The hallway and kitchen, usually so softly lit against the wood and old leather background, were aglow, every lamp and spotlight in the place blazing bright.

'Hey Grandpa!' said Greg, handing him a large bottle of Scotch. 'Why the glare?' he added, blinking.

Joseph reached for his shades.

'Oh, it's good to be dazzled,' said Theo.

That seemed to be all the Professor had to say on the matter of light bulbs. Without a further word, he went to raise the music and lower the lighting to its usual level. They assembled an antique selection of glasses and arranged themselves around the table. Heidi gazed softly at the room she loved: the battered cooking surfaces, the shelves spilling over with as many books as pots, the grand piano near the far wall, always open at the ready; the collection of strings and flutes from somewhere deep in the Amazon jungle.

'Einstein was so right,' the Professor sighed. 'The mind of God is the only thing worth knowing – oh, how I should love to know that...'

'You should try having a conversation with my mom,' suggested Heidi. 'I'll introduce you some time. That'll get you *really* wondering what goes on inside the mind of God.'

'Thanks, I may take you up on that one day: no project too large or too small. How's the week been?' he continued. 'Have you been careful with your wishes?'

'I've thought about Dorothy quite a bit,' replied Greg. 'All that passion, determination: she gets an A-grade for sticking power.'

'We took a look at the movie,' said Frank. 'Jo and I had a watch-in: two lone bachelors taking solace at Heidi's and Greg's. I see what Jo means about the paint. And what about the gypsy down the lane, the one that Dorothy rushes off to see? He feeds himself on sausages from a campfire and lives in a van: I'm not sure I buy this Wizard idea. I suppose he's quite a pleasant con man, as con men go, what with his pack of cards and general incompetence.'

'Which is the whole point, of course,' said Theo, 'and an excellent place for our girl to start her travels. Know Thyself. It's always the best way out of trouble – and a pretty good way to avoid trouble in the first place. You'd never find a way of doing that if someone else *knew thyself* for you, not that they could ever do such a thing, of course.'

'Professor Marvel seems familiar enough,' said Greg, 'as a figure: the all-powerful grown-up who really doesn't have much power at all – like the Minister or someone.'

'Church or State?' laughed Yasmin.

'Either,' said Greg. 'Or both. He's not half the duffer he pretends to be, though – kind of benevolent too.'

'Exactly,' agreed the Professor. 'So where were we last week? That kindly gypsy-professor had told Dorothy to find her way home, hadn't he, so she's made it back to her bedroom in the nick of time and now she's hurtling through the cosmos at breakneck speed.'

'With the crone, that grizzly neighbor, cackling along beside her,' said Heidi. 'Dorothy can't shake her off; the old wretch is pedaling that bike of hers as fast as she can go – and she's got hold of a broomstick and a pointed hat.'

'What's going on, then?' asked Theo. 'Why can't this brave girl escape from her troublesome stalker? You'd think if she's halfway to creating a new country, or a fresh Universe or something, disposing of a bad-tempered hag would be easy as winking.'

'She's a pretty determined hag,' said Dawn.

'And there's obviously a reason why she's staying close to Dorothy,' said Theo.

'Well,' said Greg. 'If we're pursuing last week's idea that this is a dream...'

'We aren't!' interrupted Heidi. 'I told you – Oz is a real place, and she'll soon be there!'

'A place which Dorothy has dreamed up,' said Theo. 'Just like we all dream up all our adventures, good, bad and indifferent.'

'Well, wild reverie or new location,' Greg continued, 'I'd hazard a guess that maybe the Witch is a reflection of all Dorothy's fears. Which is hardly surprising, under the circumstances. The fears, I mean.'

'Not at all surprising – and it also brings up the question of all that wishing she's been doing, doesn't it?' said their teacher. 'Or thinking, rather – which is exactly the same thing, if it's results that we're interested in.'

'Thinking is the same as wishing?' said Frank.

'Effectively, yes,' Theo replied, 'exactly the same. Be mindful what you think about; it engages the life-stream, remember.'

'OK,' agreed Frank. 'I'm getting it – engaging with it, even...'

'She's doing OK so far, though, our heroine,' the Professor continued, 'even as she brings herself, or her ego with all its

23

fears, along for the ride. She's thrown this passionate vision out to the Universe, wishing on a star, and *whoosh!* It seems like she's well on her way to creating a rather brightly lit new world – in spite of all those fear-thoughts. Not bad for day one.'

'Not bad at all,' agreed Yasmin, 'especially for someone who thinks she's got no power.'

'Quite,' said Theo. 'It's like you, Greg: your folks were set on making you into an attorney just like your old man, and what do you do? Study the human mind with an old duffer like me and start a band.'

'Oh, I live on a different planet from all of them,' said Greg. 'It's official.'

'For the moment,' agreed the Professor. 'But even the planets talk to each other in the end – in a manner of speaking.'

'Excuse me?' said Frank.

'Flashlights,' replied Theo. 'Just like the cells of your body, sending each other color-coded signals: flash, flash.'

'I've never heard that before.'

'New information, relatively speaking. Good material for another module, but the subject tonight is Oz.'

'So there goes Dorothy,' said Greg thoughtfully, 'with her reality creation – color up, so to say.'

'Exactly,' agreed Theo. 'But remember she's a learner in this game of life. There's something she's not realized. Blue skies are good, high-flying's great, but an awful lot of our dreaming comes from that dark place we were talking about last week. The place where we keep all the bits we don't know about: doubts and shame and bewilderment and fear, for instance. Hence the Witch, keeping her company.'

'I get it,' said Frank. 'The Witch *comes* from the grey zone. I've been there a time or two, I can tell you.'

'Me too,' acknowledged Joseph.

'But the hidden talents are in there too,' Theo added. 'We'll get to them later.'

'Good idea about the floodlights, then,' said Yasmin.

'Nothing wrong with a heavy hint here and there,' said the Professor. 'After all, they wrote that instruction to Know Thyself right into the stone in Delphi, in the forecourt of the Temple of Apollo, the Sun God himself.'

'And that's quite a sunny place,' said Yasmin. 'So is San Diego,' she grinned. 'Plenty of sun gods here.'

'But you can be in the warmest, most sun-god-filled place on the planet and still be dark inside,' replied the old man, 'if you don't want to look at yourself. Which most human beings don't,' he continued.

'My father would call that navel gazing,' said Greg. 'That's why he objects to me studying with an "old duffer", as you describe yourself. Narcissistic nonsense, he calls it.'

'It's exactly the opposite, of course,' replied the Professor. 'Narcissism is fully dedicated to keeping our image in place, nicely polished. And the image is the thing that we put in place to protect us from the truth we don't want to see, which is ourselves: the whole deal. With all due respect to your father, I would suggest that all the real problems in life start from our *not* looking at ourselves.'

'And he doesn't,' said Greg.

'Exactly,' agreed Theo. 'It's interesting that popping along to Delphi was all about consulting the Oracle, finding the great inside knowledge that would change the fate of nations. What's an Oracle, if it's not the voice of inner truth, I wonder?'

'I guess a lot of us wouldn't know where to begin to look for an Oracle inside,' suggested Dawn.

'No,' agreed Theo. 'So we don't do it. Problem is, when we're building our worlds from that grey zone, which is where we build them from when we *haven't* consulted the Oracle, haven't found out who we are, when we can't even *glimpse* who we really are, it's like a default setting. We slip back into a place where we don't know our power. So we create a *dis*-empowered scene for ourselves.'

'I didn't know I *had* any power,' said Joseph.

'Welcome to the human race,' Theo replied. 'You're using your power all the time, and not necessarily in a good way. Behind a carefully preserved image, most of us think we're not good enough, not clever enough, not rich enough, not worthy enough. "I'm not, I'm not, I'm not", and then – surprise, surprise – the world shows us we're right. Because we're always right – all of us!'

'Everyone?' said Yasmin. 'How does that add up? You say something's black, I say it's white; we're both right?'

'Oh yes,' said their teacher, 'because we prove to ourselves every time exactly what we want to believe. We create it through the life-energy stream. You may say something is wonderful, for instance – whatever it is – and so you'll generally find that experience proves you right, in relation to that piece, more or less. Let's imagine that I take a different view, that I believe only the worst is good enough for me. Guess what I'll get?'

'A grizzly bank balance and the neighbors from hell,' said Greg.

'That's the kind of thing,' said Theo. 'Or worse. So at the level of how we build our worlds (which we don't even realize we're doing, of course) you're right and I'm right, according to our beliefs – it's just a question of choice; of what kind of world you want to build.'

'I like this information,' said Frank, 'if it's really true. How does it work, in practice?'

'Mechanics,' answered the Prof. 'That's the bottom line. Or call it cause and effect if you prefer. You put out a thought, a belief, a feeling, into the world – or you drop them into a lake, if you like. Your thought or belief or whatever plops into the pond, just like a little pebble, and sends out ripples, or waves, on and on. Each of these thoughts is like an email addressed to the Universe, which is the energy-field we all live in, by the way. You think it,

26

the computer sends it off...'

'*Heck!*' exclaimed Joseph. 'I can feel that... Cancel this morning's thoughts – quick!'

'Cheer up,' reassured Theo. 'There are ways.'

'Phew.'

'So the Universe receives your thought-form, your imprint,' continued the Professor. 'You could say that the frequency of what you just thought about ripples to the very edge of the Universe. The cosmos, the energy-field, gets the message, or the energy squiggle, and it says, "Right, I heard you."'

'Does it have a sorting system?' asked Heidi. 'You know – something that decides, "This one's a good idea but let's bin that one"?'

'Nope,' Theo replied. 'Total freedom – it's up to you. So you send out the thought you've chosen, which takes up form as an energy squiggle, and the Universe, faithful to your every thought, sends back the exact same waveform, right to your front door. Except this time the squiggle is visible and tangible, because it shows up as a thing – or as your experience. And it may be quite an uncomfortable thing. But it's what you ordered, like a meal in a restaurant; it's a precise response to the message you sent.'

'So you mean you send out the thought that your brother's a jerk or your manager's a nightmare and they come right back and show you you're right?' asked Dawn. 'Or you're scared you'll fail the exam so they come back and give you a D-grade.'

'That's the kind of thing,' Theo replied. 'And that means that you recreate a pretty similar set-up wherever you go. You can move to a different city or a whole new country...'

'Or a new world,' suggested Heidi.

'Exactly. And you bring yourself, together with all your thoughts and fears and insecurities and doubts, along with you. So the same things come up – or back – and hit you in the face.'

'Cackling along on their bikes,' said Frank. 'I can think of a few of those.'

'So this business of light,' said Greg. 'Just to clarify: the grey zone's the place, or the state of mind rather, where we've got no power, right?'

'No *conscious* power,' the Professor agreed. 'Conscious power is the useful kind. And way more potent, by the way, than unconscious power. So chin up – we may write some less-than-ideal scripts from the grey zone – but when we get creative then wow! Do we step up the volts!''

'So the grey zone's like the default setting,' said Greg. 'The place we send messages out from when we're half-asleep, kind of thing. And the light – the Temple of Apollo and all the rest of it...'

'The light has been a metaphor for more or less everything that's good more or less since time began – so far as we know,' said Theo. 'You'll find it in every tradition: the Christians, the Jews, the Hindus, the artists. These days you'll even find it in physics: the scientists will tell you that you came from the stars, or at least that you're made of the same stuff as stars.'

'I like that,' said Greg. 'You're a star, I'm a star; we can shine however we damn well like!'

'Yes, go for it,' said Theo. 'No need for bushels and hiding places. Locking your light and talent away never served anyone. They'll tell you that light's the thing that generates all of it: plants, babies, precious stones. So at least everyone is agreed on that. They don't realize they're agreed on it, on the whole, so they'll go on finding things to argue about, of course. But light is the vital resource: you'll find it nicely separated into color-coded rays everywhere from a flowerbed to the core of your psyche – even telling *you* who *you* are, if you really want to bump up the power on your resources.'

'Psycho-spiritual floodlights,' said Yasmin. 'That could do something for the athletics teams.'

'Or any teams,' agreed their teacher. 'And individuals, come to that. It's always a good idea to bring in some extra charge, because once you get to see what's going on in the places you've never noticed inside you, you get to understand them. And understanding is power. More power.'

'So Dorothy's wandering around in the half-darkness was not such a bad plan after all,' Frank suggested. 'Plunge into that dark place and see what you find. Go hear what the Oracle says. Might even spot the personal "on" switch. Dorothy sure seems to be headed *somewhere*.'

'She is,' said Theo. 'It may take a while before she finds anything useful. That's quite normal. But she *will* find it – because the other good news is that those grey places hide a lot of other things, remember. Shine a light into your hidden corners and you find wonderful surprises: brilliance and patience, fun, the power to swap a bad mood for a good one at the drop of a hat. Maybe you see some of the amazing inventions the world hasn't even thought of yet. You know: a tune, a poem, a new use for old tires. Anything you like. It's all hidden away in the 95-odd percent of your clever minds and hearts that you've not even met yet.'

'So *that's* what's happening in Oz,' said Dawn.

'Yes,' said their teacher. 'Dorothy is waking up; she's finding out who she is when the lights go on.'

'That's quite an awesome thought,' said Frank. 'If this star theory is right, it means that finding the "on" switch is like remembering what we've forgotten, what we knew before we got caught up in the gravitational force of the grey zone. The implications are quite something.'

'They are, aren't they?' Theo replied. 'So here's the Wizard's second assignment, his next recipe for you: take a little time out this week to imagine a life, even for just a few minutes, an amazing life for yourself, which has no limitations – somewhere over the rainbow, so to speak. Kind of the opposite of a power cut.'

'In that land that we heard of, once in a lullaby,' said Yasmin.

'Quite,' said the Prof. 'Where life takes on a bit of color – unlike the Kansas half-light: you can't even *see* yourself when you're as grey as everything around you. So go search for it, go look for somewhere in your grandest visions, and try to do this more than once: do it for at least a few minutes every day. If you really knew the world – and yourselves – to be your oyster, or more exactly a source of energy and power that you could use to create any reality you choose – what are the things that you would be, do or have? In that order,' he added.

'Right now,' said Heidi, 'I'm really not too sure.'

'No, but you will be – all in good time. You each know yourself better than anyone else could ever do, remember. You just don't know that you know yourselves that well. Nobody can gainsay your greatest dreams and grandest plans – you just thought they could.'

'The dimming of the lights happens in all kinds of places, doesn't it?' said Greg. 'You don't have to be recently orphaned or manically depressed: you can be shut down just as effectively in more ordinary ways, in the mall, or the restaurant, or at the computer.'

'Just as easily,' replied the Professor. 'So give yourselves a chance, the permission to be whoever you are meant to be. Imagine that you're all-clear, all-powerful, that no-one and nothing can stand in the way of the thing you're destined to be, do *and* have. You have a special assignment – right here on this planet. No-one else can do it for you; no-one else has your particular package of talents. Believe that and the answers will come up faster than you may expect.'

'Any suggestions?' asked Heidi. 'Short cuts; ways to free up the energy flow, so we discover the hidden secrets, find out what we do want?'

'Draw it,' suggested Theo. 'Speak it, write it, cartoon it – sing about it, if you like. Stand in front of a mirror and tell yourself you can do it.'

'Make fools of ourselves, you mean,' said Joseph.

'Who says so?' asked their teacher. 'And if they do say so, the tables may turn on them, just the moment you find you really *are* doing it, whatever it is. Any or all of those things will help you get clear about where you need to go, and then to imagine it, right into being. The dream – remember? – the power of conscious dreaming. And then the dream will start to gain some substance. The spoken word, the written word, the picture: they're all part of the building job, they start to make your idea real.'

'Start, perhaps,' said Frank, the practical scientist in him kicking in as ever. 'But that *is* only a start, surely?'

'And a powerful one,' answered Theo. 'It prepares the way for action: you begin to take the actions that will make it *really* happen. But that generally comes later. Above all, trust your vision, your dream: have faith in it: there's a reason why they say faith moves mountains, you know. Believe in yourself and you can make a new world!'

'You know what?' said Joseph. 'I'm inspired. And I've not been able to say that for a while.'

'Good,' replied the Prof. 'That means you're in-spirit. Keep breathing, good and deep – that will in-spirit you some more... Have fun with it. I'll see you next week.'

Mirrors

'Now, where were we?' asked Theo the following Friday. 'Dorothy was flying through space, if I remember rightly, in that house of hers, far, far away from those dull prairies – with the Witch right beside her and a storm rocketing around them all. What happens next?'

'The storm dies down,' said Heidi, 'and everything goes calm. Dorothy glides down to land, or rather the house does. After a while she realizes the shaking really has stopped and she dares to look out of a window or open a door. And if all the color had drained out of her life before, she's about to have it made up to her with interest. Technicolor landscape or what...'

'I remember that bit,' said Frank. 'Flowers and little people all over the place. And the nasty neighbor seems to have found her come-uppance. She's been flattened by the house and all you see is a stripey-stockinged foot or two, sticking out from underneath.'

'That's right,' said Heidi, 'but then comes some shocking news: Glinda the Good Witch shows up in her floaty pink balloon and congratulates Dorothy for being a noble sorceress because she's killed the Wicked Witch. Not the accolade she's ready for.'

'Oh but there's worse to come,' said Yasmin. 'The sister arrives – a carbon copy of the first Witch – and she assures Dorothy that she'll get back at her for this. This second seething Wicked Witch has a wonderful green face,' she added gleefully.

'She would do, wouldn't she?' said Theo. 'You've heard of people being green with envy; she's jealous of anything young, innocent, anything happy. She can't seem to manage love herself, so she hates instead; she can't stand the thought of anyone else having something she hasn't got. Even though the same love would be there for the asking, for her too, if she'd only take the trouble to wake up.'

'Oh but green is beautiful!' exclaimed Yasmin. 'Come hiking with me tomorrow through the valley – I'll show you some greenery. Makes your heart sing: all that freshness, all the open space.'

'I'll pass on the hiking, thanks,' the Professor replied, with an exaggerated limp as he crossed the kitchen to fetch the steaming coffee pot. 'Bring me back some leaves, though. I love green too – and there's two sides to everything, you know.'

'Two sides to the Witches, too,' commented Heidi. 'The dead Witch lived in the West; the new one comes from the East – or maybe it's the other way around. Anyway, the nice ones hang out in the North and South.'

'Interesting, that,' said Theo.

'Why?' asked Joseph.

'She's not just being the *green monster*, that gnarled-up creature,' said the Professor. 'She's got plenty of other problems too: she's caught up in everything that keeps her out of touch with her center, her place of real power.'

'Because she doesn't know who *she* is either,' suggested Dawn, 'any more than Dorothy does – even though she's had a few more years to find out.'

'And her ego is making quite sure that she won't,' Theo agreed. 'That's what it does for all of us: it thinks we're separate from everyone and everything, so it pushes us to the edge. Worry, irritation, frustration, jealousy, rage, you name it, or you feel it, rather, and you find you're getting *beside yourself*. Not a sensible or very constructive place to be.'

'But don't worry!' said Greg. 'In comes Glinda after all, in her pastel-colored spacecraft, and she's full of all kinds of soothing advice.'

Yasmin turned to Theo. 'Maybe you'll tell me now, why you're right there with my mom?' she said. 'Grouping me in with all that pink-and-salmon floss.'

'Oh it's a great compliment she gave you,' he replied. 'Glinda from the North, supported by her sister from the South; they're great allies both – they'll help our friend keep herself upright. She'll remain a good upstanding citizen, happy and strong. Besides,' he added, 'Glinda pretty much thinks pink, wouldn't you say? She thinks and feels pretty good about life. How often d'you think Glinda would hold back from doing something in case it all goes wrong?'

'OK, she wouldn't, and it wouldn't,' agreed Yasmin. 'Go wrong,' she added.

'And you?' the Professor asked her. 'Would you hold back from doing life full-on? Would you be scared your antics would turn pear-shaped if you jumped out of an airplane with one of those umbrellas of yours?'

'She's lethal!' exclaimed Heidi. 'She tried to get me doing that parachute stunt the first day I met her. She'd get the whole world flying through the air if we let her.'

'And I've never got her up there even once,' grinned Yasmin.

'Would you hold back from helping a friend, come to that?' Theo continued, addressing Yasmin. 'Would you find reasons to hold back from that?'

'That might depend on what they want,' she replied.

'She never would, you know,' said Heidi. 'I'll tell you what, jack-in-the-box: you come into the room and we all feel better.'

'Optimism is infectious,' said Theo. 'I'd accept your mom's assessment, Yasmin, if I were you.'

'As long as I don't have to wear pink lace...'

'We'll let you off,' replied Theo. 'So here they all are, then. Dorothy seems to have disposed of one set of fears, neatly packaged up in one dead Witch and – abracadabra! – another one shows up. A bit like life, I'd say. But she's a clever kid; she's called on some higher powers, in that passionate singing of hers, so here's Glinda, the force of love, right on her new doorstep, to help her get by.'

'And the force of love, *aka* Glinda-in-frills, tells Dorothy to keep those sparkly red shoes on her feet,' said Greg. 'What's that about? Building on your green-faced theories.'

'All kinds of things,' replied the old man. 'Good, strong blood is nice and crimson; potent warmth or heat is deeply and translucently scarlet. Red will keep her vitality high, remind her to value her life, stay upbeat, be right here, right now, be a bit physical instead of living in her head, up in her dreamland...'

'So *that's* why you thought I needed those red shoes from Santa!' said Dawn. 'You were telling me I'm a dreamer.'

'Well?' said Theo. 'That's not such a bad thing, is it? I have told you never to sell out on your dreams, after all. Dreams have to be grounded, though; they have to find a form in what we call real life. First comes the idea, then you need the action. Your creativity is doing fine – always did. Meeting deadlines, not so good perhaps...'

'At least you weren't accusing me of seeing red,' she said.

'Not on the outside, anyway,' suggested the Professor, a twinkle lighting up his brow.

'I don't get angry,' said Dawn. 'If something makes me mad, I get out instead.'

'Avoiding the issue entirely,' said Frank. He was looking faintly miffed.

'There's something in this rainbow of Dorothy's,' she said, ignoring him. '"Somewhere over the rainbow" there seems to be a place where our thoughts and feelings and behaviors flash up at us in neon lighting. Providing instant feedback: neat.'

'In our dreams, it certainly seems to be neat. In this one anyhow,' said Greg.

'In our *active* dreaming,' suggested their teacher, 'or our conscious dreaming, perhaps. We did think that our heroine might possibly be dreaming. She could be meditating, of course, opening herself up to the powers of the Universe.'

'Unlikely,' said Yasmin firmly. 'The poor kid can't be more

than ten or twelve.'

'True,' said the old man. 'Though the poor kid is also every one of us, of course. Perhaps she's not dreaming, not meditating, not doing anything so abstract. You get feedback in waking life too – tends to come a bit slower. Maybe Dorothy is awake, or waking up, getting conscious, remembering her power. Maybe she's whipping up a whole new way of life, with great determination. Perhaps she's decided the last one didn't work too well so she's changing the scene, the play?'

'Maybe she's doing all of those things,' suggested Greg. 'Meditating, dream-catching, taking action...'

'If so,' said the Professor, 'she deserves an A-Star already in the game of life.'

'What, for dreaming?' grinned Dawn. 'You'll be thanking the dreamers yet.'

'For taking action!' retorted Theo. 'But I do, I do – I love the dreamers – and the dream. Where were we now?'

'Just looking at Dorothy's feet,' said Heidi, 'and finding she's been fitted out with magic shoes to keep her feet on the ground.'

'And the Wicked Witch – the one who's still alive – is trying to grab them,' said Yasmin.

'And Dorothy's decided,' added Greg, 'that all she wants is to go back home, to that dreadful place she's just escaped from. Maybe she's not quite lined up for her A-Star in life skills just yet.'

'Early days,' said Theo. '*Better the devil we know* and all that. Getting what we've wished for can be the scariest thing that ever happened. She's sure going to need those bright-red shoes, though: keep her ears to the ground, let alone her feet.'

'The slippers are silver in the book,' commented Heidi.

'Excellent for keeping in touch with her soul,' the Professor replied. 'That's what the Ancients taught us: a silver cord of light, it keeps us connected with the power. I'd give her silver *and* red both, if I were you: I'm all for bringing heaven to earth – or knowing that heaven's here already. We do tend to not notice that. At any rate, this child's got some things to tackle: let's give her all the support she can use.'

'So Dorothy is asking how to find the way home,' said Dawn, 'and Glinda and all the Munchkins – they're the little people who keep bobbing up from among the flowers – tell her she's just got to follow the Yellow Brick Road. Because if she does that, she'll find the great and wonderful Wizard, and he will have all the answers she needs: that's what they're telling her.'

'It sounds so simple,' sighed Theo. 'But *which* Yellow Brick Road? There are several, as it turns out. Ah, the poor child – she's faced with conscious choice, and no-one to help her decide.'

'Except for the Scarecrow that she meets just a few minutes after she sets out,' said Heidi. 'He knows a thing or two. Talks, too. At least he reminds her that she does have some choice in the matter, pointing his arms this way then that. And chatting to her far more than anyone ever did on the farm.'

'Just like Dawn did to me when I arrived in this place and didn't know anyone from Adam,' said Heidi. 'Hi, Scarecrow!'

'And the Scarecrow looks just like one of those farm laborers,' said Frank. 'One of the only friends she had back in the charred flatlands, apart from Toto of course. Same face, different clothes.'

'It's true then,' agreed Theo. 'You take the scary bits – the egoic, witchy bits – of yourself with you wherever you go, but you take the good bits, too. Everything in a dream, and in life, of course, is a part of yourself, a reflection.'

'Everything?' asked Frank, doubt furrowing his brow.

'In the end, yes,' said Theo. 'There's no universe without the mind, creating as it goes. Dorothy's about to discover all kinds of wonderful things about herself that she never knew, mirrored right back at her in her new-found friends. Or her old-found friends – who are showing their true colors for the first time, now that she's taken the trouble to turn the lights on.'

'That feels a bit like life as I know it,' mused Heidi. 'I can see myself in quite a few of my friends.'

'Ah!' replied Theo. 'Now you're talking! We *are* all part of each other – ask any quantum mechanic. Or a mystic. But more usefully right now, you're spot on, Heidi: our friends and families are wonderful mirrors. You could even say each of them hangs out with you so you can see a part of yourself. And you return the favor, of course. So if that's the case, let me see now, the Scarecrow would be the part of Dorothy that...'

'Thinks she's a dumb blonde,' grinned Yasmin, pulling at her sandy-colored curls.

'Familiar, though, *huh*?' smiled the Professor, looking around the table at his young friends. 'You know the times when you never think you'll make it through the oral test, or get your head around next term's module? Someone else gets the promotion, the prize – you think they're smarter than you are.'

'Just a bit,' said Dawn.

'The Scarecrow's ahead of the game, though,' said Greg. 'So cheer up, red-head: he spots the problem, finds the solution, every time. He's the brightest of the bunch.'

'Thanks,' she said.

'You're smart enough to duck and dive your way out of a certain person's grasp, anyway,' remarked Theo casually.

Frank looked up sharply.

'OK,' said the Professor boldly. 'This is a life module so let's tell it like it is. Might there be a reason, Frank, why our lovely friend here has been smart enough to protect herself from an entanglement that could end in tears?'

The younger man looked uncomfortable.

'Might it have something to do with another character who soon shows up in Dorothy's little drama?' continued their teacher, looking warmly at his student. 'That Cowardly Lion, the one who thinks he's got no courage, never dives in, never really shows up for what he is, until these good friends of his force the issue: they invite him to come along with them and find the

Wizard.'

'OK,' said Frank, bracing himself. 'I feel an assignment coming.'

'I'm thinking it might be worth your while taking a little look at how you do relationships – a toe in here, a foot in there... A little trail of broken hearts behind you, or annoyed ones?'

'I don't set out to hurt anyone,' said Frank.

'I believe you,' answered Theo. 'The road to hell – or chaos, perhaps – is paved with good intentions, but underneath the road you sometimes find rocky foundations: a bit of frost here, an emotional storm there, and the paving stones start to crack.'

'I guess they have done sometimes,' said Frank. He colored warmly, silent for a few moments.

'It's not unusual,' Theo continued. 'We all have good intentions that crack.'

'I've never really thought about why it happens,' said Frank, 'whenever I hook up with someone. The first bit's so easy, then it gets tricky and I scat. Bad habit.'

'And the question is why,' continued the Professor gently. 'We all know you're a bright spark; you don't look too bad either,' he added. 'There's something you're scared of, too scared to allow anyone to come real close. No wonder you've put so much of yourself into your work. Paid off, too, in that area.'

'That's the easy part,' said Frank. 'Work's a doddle.'

'Work is just a word,' said Theo. 'It's a label we use for certain categories of activity; often we think they're a slog, but they are the things we expect to get rewarded for – they bring us money, for instance, or useful knowledge. Working on ourselves is no different; it's a slog, and we get rewarded for it.'

'Why do we go to such lengths to avoid what we think of as work, then?' Frank asked.

'Oh it's just fear that makes us lazy,' Theo replied cheerfully. 'It makes us forget how smart we are. Look at you – you can be just as competent in other pieces of your life as you are in your studies: you need to look in the mirror and see what's really going on in that heart of yours. The Lion's King of the Jungle, remember?'

'Except when he's got no guts,' said Frank, staring at the coffee grains in his empty cup.

'Or when he believes that he has, which is nothing more than a fiction,' said his teacher.

Dawn was silent, thinking about the way Frank had taken care of his younger sister since she'd arrived in town last year: the cash handouts, the introductions, the vigilance, the meals, the hugs. The big brother from heaven.

'So those are two of Dorothy's friends, two of her mirrors, already,' Theo continued. 'The Scarecrow and the Lion. Who else was there? There was the one who showed up before the Cowardly Lion came roaring out of the wood, wasn't there?'

'The Tin Woodman,' said Yasmin. 'Joseph's double – well, used to be, until about last Thursday when Jo came back to life. The Tin Woodman is all creaky and sad. He fell in love and was revving up for marriage and happily ever after, so the Wicked Witch came along and chopped out his heart. Now he's convinced he's missing that vital organ so there's no juice left in his veins, his joints are stiff as rusty hinges, he's all seized up, he'll never love again.'

'Oh dear,' said Greg. 'He's *really* lost heart, hasn't he?'

'*Mm*,' agreed Theo. 'All the color washed right out of his life.'

'I know the feeling,' Joseph said, a rueful grin spreading across his face.

'Especially the feeling that he'll never *be* loved again,' added Yasmin. 'Funny how he never even noticed that everyone's just crazy about him...'

'Or that his feelings blaze from his pores and shine from his eyes and run down his cheeks, plain for all to see,' said Dawn.

'So we've got a brainless Scarecrow with quick wits and a loveless Tin Woodman with his heart on his sleeve,' remarked

Frank, 'or his tin arm. And a lame Cowardly Lion with ex-girlfriends left behind in the woods,' he added.

'Not lame,' Theo disagreed, 'just remembering how to walk again. And you'll find that our friend the King of the Jungle is about to reclaim his sovereignty anyway. Everything we need is right inside us. Sometimes takes a little finding... Upshot is we look for something on the outside to convince us that it's there at all – which means we can help each other enormously, of course.'

'We show one another all kinds of things,' suggested Greg. 'Some of them pretty, some not so much.'

'You've hit the nail on the head,' agreed Theo.

'And they're color-coded, these traits?' Greg asked.

'In the story they are,' said Theo. 'Color is just a flashlight – it can alert us to how we're doing with the life-stream, if we're smart. *See red* – in other words indulge your anger and resentment or your fears around survival, for instance – and you contract, you shut down the flow. Feel the passion and power and some of the awesome opportunities carried on the life-stream, and you expand, you *engage* the flow.'

'What a huge and wonderful thought!' said Dawn.

'So of course you can be yellow-bellied or sunny,' Theo continued. 'You can be green with envy, or take a leaf out of nature's book and swell your heart. You can get an attack of the blues or be one of Dorothy's happy bluebirds – peaceful as they come. Choice, you see.'

'But what did Greg mean about our showing each other things?' asked Joseph.

'We run up against other people,' Theo replied, 'and first we may think we like those other people – he's funny, she's cute, they're smart. Then we start working with them, or living with them. We get to know them better; we see behind the glass, in a manner of speaking. They start to annoy us, or upset us, or undermine us.'

'Not Dorothy's other people, though,' said Yasmin. 'They're

having a ball. Once they know which yellow road to follow, the party never stops.'

'You're right,' said Theo. 'Once they stop feeling yellow-bellied and go for it. Well there's no time-lag in dreams, or stories – let's imagine they've folded all the time they needed to get the uncomfortable pieces out of the way. In Oz, they've forgotten the frictions and bumps that come between close friends, house-mates, workmates, married couples – whoever – so they just get on with it and be happy, right there, right then. We'll get there ourselves, one of these days.'

'We need a leg up, though,' said Frank.

'Here's our Wizard's next assignment, then,' replied Theo. 'Find some of the mirrors in your own lives: your mom, your brother, your used-to-be best friend. Any of your traveling companions will do. Imagine they're right there with you, warts and beauty spots and all, and notice the ways that underneath the surface, there are well-disguised parts of them that are very much like you.'

'Or well-disguised parts of us that are very much like them,' suggested Frank.

'That's it,' said Theo. 'It's not always a comfortable process, this one, but oh, it's so well worth it, especially when you start to see how smart you are, how brave and big-hearted and resourceful and wise. We'll see each other again in exactly seven days' time – or well before then, perhaps, if you catch sight of me in the mirror…'

The Yellow Brick Road

The pale golden sand stretched almost as far as the eye could see in both directions, undulating through the rough dunes around the bay, as waves crashed wildly against the rocks of the vast ocean. A long rainy season had left the landscape glistening and damp: a pod of dolphins played in the distance; the odd cormorant skimmed across the surface of the water, but otherwise they had the place almost to themselves.

Heidi ran her hand through the sand.

'This is the yellow road I love,' she said. 'I'll miss it, you know, all of it – if I do leave, that is.'

'You'll miss it for a while,' Theo replied, 'But you'll be OK, you know – good beaches back East; bracing winters; great seafood...'

'Yeah, and no old duffers. It's you I'll miss the most. I mean Greg will still be *there*, somehow, even if I'm in Boston, but you belong here.'

'Cheer up,' he said. 'It will be way worse for me: there's the tragedy of my life, watching my best-loved fledglings fly away to other planets.'

Heidi glanced quietly at her teacher. The usual glint played around his eyes.

'Of course, I might not even *go* back East,' she continued. 'I have to get a few things straight in my mind, find that road of yellow bricks. It may be heading off in some other direction entirely.'

They sat in silence a while, undisturbed by any sound save the birds and the rhythmic roar of the surf. The old man reminded Heidi of her own father in more ways than one: even his profile, with the great Roman nose and the high forehead, had a strange similarity to the man etched in her childhood memories.

'When did you start feeling like Dorothy?' Theo asked her gently. 'When do you think that really all began?'

'Hey, you've got the lasers on again tonight, haven't you?' she laughed.

'Ah, but the real trick is to see in the dark,' he replied. 'Not that it's dark yet, anywhere near. Dear heaven, how I love the spring! So when, about?'

'I guess long before my dad died,' she said. 'He'd checked out years before, really. When he made his final exit, that left me, my mom, and that brother of mine.'

'And when your dad checked out, so to say, earlier on – you would have been, what, eleven?'

'Twelve, maybe,' she said. 'Thirteen, even.'

'Well,' said Theo, 'you can't start too soon, you know, on this trip.'

'This trip where, though?' she asked. 'You're not talking holiday destinations.'

'No,' admitted her mentor. 'It's more the destiny kind of destinations that loom large at present, isn't it?'

'Something like that,' she replied. 'All that subtle pressure: it's kind of hard to go anywhere, even to inner places. My mom's psychotic, I swear it.'

'So when your dad gave up on it all, you found yourself in Kansas.'

'Too right,' Heidi agreed.

'A not-so-subtle shade of grey. I'd award you a diploma for mental health, under the circumstances. Your old man gave you some nifty gifts before he quit.'

'I guess he did,' she said. 'He took the trouble to listen, like you do. Later on, he turned into a kind of Professor Marvel in my mind, or the Wizard or something. He always appeared to have the answers I needed, if only I could get a hold of him. Kind of never there when I wanted him, so I was always looking for him in my head or my heart, waiting for the next time he cheered up

– or even showed up.'

'Hard for him to show up for you when he couldn't even show up for himself, you know,' said Theo gently. 'None of us can do that.'

'I guess,' she agreed. 'As I got older, he didn't seem all-powerful like he did in the early days. He had lots of ideas so he was great to talk to. Applying them didn't happen so much...'

'Ideas are the easy bit. Putting them into practice, not so easy – comes later for all of us, if it comes at all!'

They were silent a while, listening to nothing but the movement of the waves, rhythmically washing fresh supplies of kelp from the rich ocean forests right onto the shore, almost at their feet.

'Dorothy managed to whip up the world of her dreams,' Heidi went on. 'But then she got there and wanted out. *I want to go ho-o-o-me!* She said it often enough. I sometimes feel the same way – worrying about the folks back East.'

'And you may remember that Professor Marvel has advised Dorothy that home is where she's best headed for, even before the journey has even begun. But you don't suppose he meant that literally, do you? You don't really think he was urging her to go back to square one and spend her life on a piece of parched earth?'

'No,' Heidi conceded. 'Home has far more potential than that... I guess I'm just looking for a way to get there, wherever it might be. Greg lives and breathes music. Frank's got his job with that new energy company, Yasmin'll be busy training athletes, even Jo's OK; his joints will soon be oiled again, so to speak. He can study for the next ten years if he likes, with family backing like his – and he's pretty passionate about creating spaces.'

'And Dawn?'

'She'll do something wonderful, she can't help it – whatever she may think about *not good enough*! I guess she'll combine all her skills, one way or another: acting, dancing, the lot. She'd be a great teacher, for starters.'

'Oh she'll be creative, all right. And so, my dear girl, will you. A journey of a thousand miles starts with a single step – old Chinese proverb. In Oz, of course, that means the first yellow brick. Step on and away you go.'

'*Hmm*,' she murmured.

'You've got a good ally in that Gregory friend of yours, too. Now there's a man who will beat his own drum. And stand beside you while you beat yours.'

'Hey!' called Greg cheerfully, clambering over a rock towards them, followed by the rest of the group. 'I hope you remembered not to say a single interesting thing before we arrived,' he added.

'Not a word,' said the Professor. 'We've been boring each other to sobs, basking on the sand. It's soft, it's even getting warm.'

'We've been slaving away in the deli,' Greg replied, 'racking our brains around olives, tomatoes, cheese... Scarecrow pointed us every which way.'

'Choice,' added Dawn, as they set drink cans and bulging food-bags on the rug.

'So it's back to work, then,' said Theo. He broke the bread loaf that Frank handed him and offered the pieces around. 'Before this evening light begins to fade. Where were we last week?'

'We were looking in the mirrors,' said Joseph.

'Indeed we were,' agreed the old man. 'There was quite an array of mirrors, nicely arranged along that yellow road, if I remember rightly, in the faces of that little crowd of Scarecrows and Lions. As well as along the roads of your own great and noble lives, of course,' he added.

'Whose roads aren't too obviously yellow, as far as I can see,' said Frank. 'Or if so, I hadn't noticed.'

'Oh but they are,' Theo replied. 'Far more yellow than you may imagine. Think of all the bright and shiny things that show up around you. Yellow sunlight, yellow stars, spring flowers: all that vitality and fresh young life – it never stops. Look at all the new opportunities, all the chances that come along for you to shine a bright light and be yourself – just like the bright-gold sun in a blue sky. Now *there's* a thing with no worries about being its own person – it sparkles and shines the day away whenever it feels inclined to declare itself.'

'That would be nice,' mused Dawn.

'Go for it, then,' Theo replied. 'By the powers invested in me by the Munchkins, I hereby grant you permission to shine.'

'Hear, hear!' said Frank. 'Actually I thought she was already doing so, 24/7.'

'Beauty is in the eye of the beholder,' said Greg.

'And beholders are most excellent mirrors,' added Theo.

'So this road of Dorothy's is yellow because... ?' asked Yasmin. 'I mean, it could be bright red, or orange or something.'

'Because yellow's your own personal sun-spot, for one thing,' said Theo. 'A bright light does encourage you to develop your *own* light, forge your own path. Not that *that's* all easy, mind: it can be quite scary.'

'So the yellowness of that sunny road drops hints about our route to getting out there, does it – into the big, wide world?' said Joseph.

'It does,' the Professor replied, 'and also *in* there – to that most useful place right inside you. It shows the way home, in fact. The journey provides all kinds of delightful, sun-filled opportunities, along with its not inconsiderable hazards, which are enough to make the best of us feel more than a little weak at the knees.'

'What kinds of hazards?' asked Yasmin. 'It looks like fun to me.'

'All sorts,' said Theo. 'There's "not good enough", for instance, "not clever enough". There's this little thing we call ego, otherwise known as the Wicked Witch: it's the part of every one of us that's wired into the set-up to make us believe that we're each separate from our fellow man. The ego cons us into thinking small and scarce, so we shut down our real power and grab what little pieces we can find instead – from each other, generally, rather than the great Universal well.'

'Our egos muscle in when the journey's getting tough, don't they?' suggested Greg. 'And they often overplay their role, upset the apple cart.'

'What is the ego's role, then?' asked Yasmin. 'In a good way, I mean?'

'Thanks, Glinda!' said Theo. 'Always good to start with the plus side. So, let's see now: it gets you out there, the ego. And it gives you some necessary boundaries. You need those to navigate life safely.'

'And then it overdoes them,' suggested Heidi. 'Is that the main problem?'

'Pretty much,' agreed their teacher. 'The ego creates walls around the heart – around all kinds of things, in fact. And all because of its idea that it's on its own. In the end this is not true, as it turns out – but it's a useful thing to believe for a while, as that belief forces you to find your own way, to discover your special brand of brilliance. Therein lie some of the dangers, of course... the Wicked Witch gets up to her old tricks. Makes you think your ego's *it*. Most disempowering.'

'And the old Witch leaves annoyed hearts behind her,' said Frank, 'or behind him. I've done some mirror work this week. Uncomfortable. Very useful.'

'Congratulations,' grinned Theo. 'Braveheart, confounding the ego. It does so love to stop us from seeing through the looking-glass, you know.'

'It keeps us staring *at* it instead!' laughed Dawn.

'That's *exactly* what it does,' confirmed Theo.

'I heard a good acronym for the ego,' said Greg. '"Edging God Out".'

'Whatever God is,' said Frank.

'It's OK as a name,' said Greg. 'A good word for all kinds of things: the life-force, the Creator, the Universal Mind...'

'That kind of thing,' agreed Theo. 'And the poor old ego does have a way of swinging from a collapsed balloon state to an over-inflated one; finds it hard to stay in the middle, so it tries to stay in control, it decides it's extra-good, extra-clever, arrogant as you please; it'll move into greed, maybe. But then it swings the other way and tells us a different story; in fact it will go to some lengths to persuade us that because we're all alone we're really very small and unsafe.'

'Well, we are, aren't we?' said Joseph. 'We're alone – that's for sure.'

'Yes, but not really,' agreed the Professor. 'We're alone but we're not. And unsafe? Well, that depends on how we feel, I guess. Which side of the bed we got out on that day, for instance.'

'That's true,' said Dawn. 'When things are going well I feel secure as houses. But the feeling can change to heeby-jeebies in a flash: all it takes is a bad mark...'

'Or a phone call from Boston,' added Heidi.

'And the ego's delighted,' said Theo. 'It takes so little to keep this little entity well-fed on scary meals, or depressed ones, guilt-laden ones, worried ones – it's all the same. All those states of mind make their own road blocks,' he added. 'It's a tricky customer, the ego, and well worth knowing. It's very nicely illuminated when the yellow lights go on. We can't get anywhere very much without it, as we were just agreeing – we rely on it entirely to take us out into the world, to do our thing.'

'Meeting our mirrors as we go,' said Yasmin. 'I do see your point,' she added, looking at their teacher. 'They're not always *completely* comfortable...'

'How did your assignment go then? Anything useful in the mirrors?'

'I found I was just as impatient as my sister! And just as crazy about winning as those not-always-gorgeous kid tennis players I'm coaching. Are those things such a good idea? Impatience, competitiveness; I'm not so sure...'

'Yes,' replied the old man. 'Or no, of course, depending what you do with them. For impatience you could read motivation – depends how you behave. And I like the one about Jesus at the football match – cheering both sides at once, enjoying the game. Did anyone else meet any handy mirrors?'

'I did,' said Frank. 'I found I was just as scared as those ex-girlfriends of mine – and that my heart was annoyed too, about a few things.'

'And I discovered I could do manipulation and control with the best of them,' added Joseph. 'I could compete with Kate herself... Bit of a shock.'

'So our roads are just as yellow as Dorothy's,' laughed Heidi. 'We're all yellow-bellied and we don't even notice.'

'Oh yes,' said Theo. 'The angst is all in there – hiding in the yellow bricks, or in you. But I guess we can be as impatient as we like – or competitive – if it gets us where we need to be without knocking anything over on the way. And sometimes just as scared even, if it urges us to pull ourselves up a peg or two.'

'How about that yellow thing is the path that the Wizard has already set for Dorothy's ego to travel along?' asked Greg thoughtfully. 'Perhaps it's a set-up – a bit like life – where her ego feels the fears and tries to keep her small, but she does what she has to anyway. Perhaps her storyline, the trail of events that make her little history, is set up so she develops a solid sense of identity? She couldn't do *that* back in Kansas!'

'That's how it works,' said Theo. 'The events are the stuff of all our stories, but the problem starts when we get stuck with them and start thinking that the stories *are* us, instead of just something that influences us.'

'*Yikes!*' said Dawn. 'I've done that for years. I *am* my story! I could have sworn it...'

'And so runs the age-old fiction,' Theo replied. 'We think our stories run us when really it's the other way around. So it's just as well that we're always free to change the story, start writing a better one. The ego loves the *old* stories, the his-tories, her-stories. The ego *comes* from the past, you see – it's always busy, busy, remembering old wounds and fears, the feelings of being a little island, all on its own.'

'And it has to survive,' said Frank. 'Or it thinks it does.'

'That's right,' agreed the Professor. 'So it feeds on old stresses and anxieties, skimming over the surface of life from the past to the future – rather like that cormorant is doing out there.'

'Except the cormorant dives when it needs food,' said Dawn.

'Which is exactly what we have to do,' answered Theo. 'We have to dive into what's here and what's now. The moment, the present, the presence: get some *real* food. When we do that, something amazing happens: the Wicked Witches can't pull us East or West, because we're standing in our power. Right in the middle of it.'

'But to even begin to find that power,' suggested Heidi, 'you have to find a sense of identity first.'

'And there lies the rub,' said Theo. 'That's why the Yellow Brick journey has to happen for us, too. The ego gives us a pathway towards something that eventually takes us beyond the limitations of its little self, you see. It takes us to a far softer and more expansive space – in the end. And if we're willing to go there.'

'That's awesome,' said Greg. 'It's like a road that leads us from ego-power to soul-power; battery-power to mains electrics.'

'So where is the Yellow Brick Road leading *to*?' asked Frank. 'Where's it going? Really.'

'Ah,' replied the Professor. 'It leads to the very heart of the matter! But maybe we should make a move – the sun's gone in, the air is cooling fast; my joints are beginning to creak. Thank you for that most delicious evening meal.'

'Any chance of an assignment this week?' asked Frank. 'I need one.'

'Me too,' said Yasmin. 'This Kansas kid is smart.'

'That's easy, then,' Theo replied. 'Take a look at the Yellow Brick Roads of your own: the ones that have led you to just the place you're in now. Look back at the twists and the turns in your lives, at the apparent coincidences, and begin to notice how perfect they have been every step of the way – even when they looked like the opposite. You will start to find that very little has happened by chance after all. Eventually the picture starts to look like a beautiful tapestry taking shape behind you – perfect in every stitch.'

'Which is certainly far from obvious at the time you're in it,' said Heidi, 'living it.'

'Far from obvious,' agreed Theo. 'And that is why I'm sure the Wizard would highly recommend this little discipline, looking back from time to time at the amazing perfection of your life, as lived so far. It provides excellent training in the business of claiming your vital role as an artist, you see, because you begin to see how skilled you were before you even thought you picked up any skills.'

'Like refusing to go to Harvard and finishing up here in the sun,' said Greg.

'Or breaking my arm last year so I *had* to stop playing around and do some study...' added Yasmin.

'Exactly,' said Theo. 'Builds up your confidence, your creative talent, no end, seeing how neatly you plotted it out after all. Besides, the powers that be like nothing more than a spot of gratitude. See the perfection, say a big thank you; even more perfection comes wafting over your way.'

'So Greg was right?' Heidi said. 'The path, with all its hazards and all its fun, was a set-up organized by the Wizard – ahead of time?'

'Oh yes, it most certainly was,' said Theo. 'You remember what I said a few weeks back: that you'd be meeting the old boy soon enough? He's been there all the way along, you see, looking after you even when you thought you were all alone.'

'Who is this Wizard?' said Dawn. 'He keeps himself so private.'

'Ah well,' the old man replied. 'We shall soon get to know him a little better. He always reveals himself in the end.'

The Emerald City

'I do love a good bourbon,' said Theo, handing the golden liquid around the table. 'It warms the cockles of the heart. Just as well, I'd say, since we're headed for the Emerald City: you can't be sure they'll let you in first time, you know…'

They were back in their usual Friday-evening location. The table was littered with brightly colored sketches and rough paintings: yellow roads winding through deep-green forests; thick rays of gold-white light beaming down through the trunks of trees, deep into the earth. Glowing scenes of fairies and flowers shone out from the rough pages; they almost seemed to light up the room.

'You're a dark horse,' said Joseph. 'I never knew you could make these enchanted forests with just a simple paintbox.'

'We're all artists,' Theo replied. 'I told you so, remember?'

'You've captured the magic of Dorothy's woodlands,' said Heidi. 'It's friendly and scary all at the same time.'

'Like life,' said the Professor. 'Or like that yellow road through life that we were talking about last week. Has your week's journey been a pleasant one? Sunny and smooth; not too many hazards on the way?'

'None at all,' said Heidi. 'The music company gave Greg a contract: he's headed for the Golden Gate up North. Thanks for the Bourbon – it's right on!'

'Hey,' said Theo, patting Greg's shoulder. 'That's grand. Even your old man might start hearing you now…'

'I wouldn't be too hopeful,' said Greg cheerfully. 'But guess what? Take a look at Dawn there, sitting so quiet. She's applied for her Master's degree!'

'Well, there's a big step,' replied Theo. 'And she'll come through with flying colors. *There* are some major road blocks shifted.'

'Like our heroine in Oz, maybe,' replied Dawn happily.

'Oh yes,' said Theo, 'she's made friends with herself too – well, with her companions; it's much the same thing. Shouldn't be long now before she makes it to that green-walled place she's headed for.'

'Where the great and powerful Wizard is widely believed to hang out,' added Frank.

'Quite, quite,' agreed the old man. 'How does the saga go, then? Heidi, my dear: can you fill us in a little, please? Tell us something about our young friend's journey to the Emerald City, perhaps?'

'Well,' said Heidi, 'the Witch has a glass ball gizmo – it picks up satellite pictures of what they're all doing so she knows just how to trip them up. And when and where of course. So she whips up some bright-red poison poppy fields, from the stronghold of her castle. They have to negotiate those before they'll get any further.'

'Ah,' said Theo. 'Red alert, indeed! The flesh and the red blood.'

'What?' asked Yasmin. 'I'm missing a link.'

'The distractions of the material world, my dear. All too easy to get overly preoccupied with the concerns of the body – or its pleasures, of course. Our heroine had better remember to look up as well as down. We get lazy, don't we, on our journeys?'

'So that's why Glinda sends in the snow powder!' exclaimed Dawn. 'It's to help her clean up, revitalize, reconnect her light.'

'Precisely,' he said.

'In the book,' commented Heidi thoughtfully, 'they have to find their way across a raging river as well as those dreaded poppy fields. That's quite a thing too.'

'Oh it is, it is. There's nothing like the churning of emotions – the ones we've not sorted. They'll drown you if you don't take care. Envy, hatred, self-pity, despondency, resentment, shame: you name it, it'll bar the way to the Emerald City every time,' he sighed.

'I'd never thought of emotions as being dangerous,' Greg commented quietly.

'Only sometimes,' Theo replied. 'In good shape, they're an invaluable source of power, as Dorothy is about to discover when she reaches... Oh do remind us, Heidi. Where *is* it that she reaches, and what does she find there?'

'It gets pretty cheerful – for a time,' Heidi said. 'They reach this green, green, *green* place and the doorkeeper reluctantly lets them in. It's a proper funfair inside: people in fancy costumes, fairytale carriages pulled along by horses.'

'Which aren't green,' commented Dawn. 'Funny thing, that: the horses keep changing color – pink, purple, gold.'

'You see,' said Theo. 'Emotions in harmony and abundance – and graceful, fluent flow. Invaluable, as we just agreed.'

'Water and horses *both* stand for emotions, do they?' asked Greg. 'In this heavily symbolic Universe she's conjured up.'

'Oh yes,' Theo replied. 'And in our own – since the most ancient times: untamed, emotions are just like wild horses, running crazy, causing all kinds of chaos, outside as well as in. But when they're tamed, what friends they do become! We have to open the doors of our hearts, of course, if we want to make friends of these emotions – otherwise they'll churn us up and batter us around and make us most uncomfortable.'

'I'd make friends with horses of any color,' said Yasmin happily. 'They remind me of the funfair.'

'When you felt what?' asked Theo. 'Happiness, peace of mind...'

'Yes, both of those,' she replied. 'And gratitude – loads of it. And love of beauty, I guess – you know, the sunshine, the happy faces. Love of life.'

'Which meant that everything flowed along nicely,' said the Professor. 'Or trotted, perhaps, rather as it does in the heart of this exotic place. So they've made it to the Emerald City, then, our young friends – do they get to see His Great Highness the Wizard?'

'Not yet,' said Heidi. 'They go into the green room, so to say, to get their costumes fixed. Hairdos, facelifts, stuffings – whatever it takes.'

'Sounds like putting on your Sunday best for church,' suggested Greg.

'Hey, but perhaps it is,' said Dawn quietly. 'Not such a bad idea, lifting ourselves up by the bootstraps, being the best we can be on the outside. Helps the inside, don't you think?'

'Oh indeed,' replied Theo. 'It most certainly does. Does the Wizard welcome them into his tabernacle, then, his inner temple?'

'No!' said Frank. 'They get to see an optical illusion and hear a booming voice that scares them nearly witless. And the booming voice sends them away again, tells them they've got to kill the Wicked Witch before he, or it, rather, will give them their brains or their courage – or anything at all, in fact.'

'Ah,' sighed Theo. 'Like life, then. We work and work, we go up hill and down dale, cope with all kinds of difficulties. We pass the exam, find the dream mate at last, or the job. *Whew,* we think, *we've made it! We can clock off now, have some down time!* Well deserved, we believe.'

'Which it is,' said Joseph. 'Trust me!'

'Oh I know, I know,' sighed Theo. 'Trouble is, there's always more to be done: shadow work, finding the pieces of ourselves that are still hiding, running us from their place in the dark. We've still to dig around a bit if we're to find our great magnificence and glory. Otherwise we just might end up as victims, and that would never do.'

'Dorothy's done well, though,' said Joseph. 'She's edged open the door into that Emerald City. Her sunny road seems to have shown her the way there, at least.'

'True,' said the Professor. 'She's made an excellent start. You see what we mean about that rather delightful yellow road? The ego gets us out into the world, despite its annoying little traits. It's thanks to that me-centered, world-centered self that we go exploring at all. We meet the hazards and yes, for sure, the wily ego will try to keep us small and meek, shut us down.'

'Like some of our relations, too,' said Greg. "Don't go!" they yell. "Don't leave me! How will I ever get by without all that fear to feed on, all the lovely control and stress and angst that binds us together? It's the only food I can digest!"'

'Quite so,' agreed their teacher. 'We should feel thoroughly sorry for egos everywhere. They live on such a sad diet. But the path, or the adventures on the path, do the very opposite of contracting us down. They give us exactly what we need to expand, to grow. They lead us right to the Emerald City itself.'

'Which is what, exactly?' asked Frank.

'The heart, my friend,' replied Theo, 'the heart.'

'Just checking,' Frank said. 'Funny that it's painted green.'

'Not really,' said the Professor. 'Green is the balance color at the center of the rainbow, after all, and we surely need to be centered in that heart-place if we wish to be stable, don't we? It's a good place to reach out from, like trees do, stretching their arms to meet the world, all ways at once.'

'Nature's pretty much all green,' remarked Dawn.

'And nature is expansive, by her very *nature*,' suggested Theo. 'Abundant, prolific, far-reaching, ever-giving, ever-receiving – straight from the fountain of the great Source itself.'

'So you mean that as we get in touch with our own hearts,' said Greg, 'we can expand and surpass ourselves, in the journey along the road. And life gets *better*.'

'Exactly so,' said Theo. 'Opening our hearts is the most useful thing we can ever do. Not easy – spiritual traditions have been working on the problem for a few millennia – but entirely necessary. Each little crack of light that seeps into the heart is a step in the right direction. Enlightened self-interest, I'd call it, persuading our hearts to wake up after all those ego-layers have bundled them up so thoroughly, kept them in the dark. Cracks of sunshine and warmth – oh my...'

'Why does that "green" door get shut in the first place?' asked Heidi.

'It's called forgetfulness,' Theo replied. 'And it's an entirely necessary part of our exploring that yellow road and everything it leads to. Come into the world, shut the door behind you to wherever it was you were before, go adventuring. When you've explored enough, you'll need to find that door again – but you'll have some invaluable experience to take back through it with you.'

'Like in Narnia,' said Greg.

'Quite true,' agreed Theo. 'Then in comes the warmth, the light, as you open it – and the heart sparks up with delight, putting you back in touch with who you are, re-membering you, connecting you with the awesome power of love that comes from your higher self.'

'I'm feeling that light, that movement, as you speak,' said Frank. 'It's like a little bulb has been switched on inside my chest and I'm sensing some movement.'

'Quick work, Frank!' said their teacher. 'I said you could do nifty work in plenty more ways than one.'

'This is amazing!' said Heidi. 'I can feel it too. What *is* that sensation of energy here, right in the middle of my chest?'

'Oh it's a wonderful organ, the heart,' replied Theo. 'Starts beating all of its own accord, you know, before the brain even thinks about getting started – before you even *have* a brain. Begins life, maintains it, even ends it. The ancient Trinity of life itself: "Generates, Operates, Destroys".'

'G-O-D,' murmured Heidi.

'As above, so below,' agreed Theo. 'Makes sense, doesn't it?' he added. 'One of the greatest Teachers of all time, J. Christ himself, made rather a point of letting us know that the very Kingdom of

G-O-D is inside us, after all. If there's a doorway to that happy state of being, I would imagine the heart is by far the most likely place to find it.'

'It's a comforting thought,' said Greg. 'We can open the flood-gates to a force that pumps light to all our cells. Kind of oxygen with some extras.'

'Which were there all along – the extras – only we didn't notice them,' Theo replied. 'So you see,' he continued, 'the heart knows exactly what it's doing – and what *we* are doing. It has brain cells inside it; it can think. You can't fool your heart, you know: it always knows better.'

'So that's why we feel uncomfortable inside when we screw up,' said Joseph.

'That would be it,' agreed Theo. 'Our monkey brains can play all kinds of tricks, sitting there aloft in the tops of the trees, bobbing around in our heads like a great big apple, thinking they're above it all so they run the show. They don't, you know. They're very good at mental gymnastics, of course. But our hearts are deep inside our bodies, right at the core. They've got the leverage: insider knowledge.'

'So our hearts know the truth,' said Yasmin, 'don't they? They know when we mess up, when we're not being true to ourselves, but they know who we are, and what we stand for and even where we're meant to be headed, maybe? So they will remind us of it. The heart must be a proper Aladdin's Cave, full of goodies!'

'Ah!' laughed Theo. 'So that's why Aladdin was your favorite story.'

'No,' insisted Yasmin. 'The flying carpet was the thing.'

'I see your point about our all being artists,' said Dawn. 'There's a whole storehouse of useful resources inside us, isn't there? I like that.'

'So do I,' agreed the old man, 'and there's even more to like: the heart is a kind of engine house. That Emerald green place can draw on all the resources of the Universe, because it's properly wired up to them. The heart is like a satellite station, receiving signals – sending them out, connecting with everything every-where – and doing the same with all kinds of energy, connecting with the light. Nature does this clever thing with light, you know: it takes it and converts it into leaves.'

'*Oh wow!*' said Yasmin. 'I'd never thought of that. We *eat* light.'

'And isn't it delicious?' said Theo. 'Have some lettuce,' he added, reaching for a bowl of salad from the side. 'And rocket, and spinach – whatever you like. The heart does something really rather similar, you see, in your own life. It absorbs the energy of the Universe; it takes in all of your experience, and it transforms it – usually into something very handy.'

'Like wisdom, for instance,' suggested Heidi.

'And discrimination, and gratitude, and creativity,' added Theo.

'Joy, even,' said Dawn. 'And love, of course.'

'All of that,' agreed Theo, 'and more.'

'The heart-engine-house!' exclaimed Greg. 'What does it do? How does it work? Apart from the obvious, I mean, pumping all that blood around, sending it out to the extremities of our bodies and bringing it back home for refueling.'

'And sending us out to the furthest edges of our experience and bringing us back home for refueling!' added Theo.

'So that's why the Wizard sends them away!' exclaimed Heidi. 'They have to go off and get *really* tested – do the extreme stuff – before they're ready to bring it all back home; to bring back all their experience.'

'I suspect that's exactly the reason,' said Theo. 'And there's a few more things we have to learn yet about our hearts. But enough is enough. I shall answer your question next week, Gregory, dear boy. It's one that's well worth pondering.'

'Thank you,' said Greg. 'Emeralds have long been prized for some kind of inner value as well as for being very nice to look at. Some legends have said the Holy Grail itself was made of

Emerald, I've been told.'

'Yes indeed,' Theo agreed. 'So how about you all go off now and gather up some more experience. I shall sit in the grass, or on the sand, and reflect upon the Emerald City. You can go and see if anyone's offering you any more contracts, or Master's degrees.'

'Or face a few raging rivers or poppy fields!' suggested Heidi.

'Oh I do hope not,' said Theo. 'Although they do stimulate some interesting events along the way. Emotions are rather useful if you really want to get to know the wonderful potential that's lying dormant in your heart, just waiting to be sparked into life. Make friends with those emotions – even the difficult ones. They just may hold the fuel for your transformation.'

His creased and wizened face twinkled as they headed for the door.

'Not forgetting,' he added, 'that you are perfect exactly as you are. Never let anyone persuade you otherwise!'

The Inner Temple

The fresh season was expanding its light and warmth every day. New growth was everywhere: that was the good news for Heidi who always loved the spring. But with it came the last push towards the impending exams: that was the bad news.

Thank God it's Friday, she thought as they mounted the steps to Theo's front door.

'Come into the garden,' he said, smiling broadly. 'It is my Inner Temple, and only available when Apollo wills it so. I hope you've been enjoying the sunshine.'

He led them through a maze of corridors to a plain wooden door at the back of the house. Taking a large iron key from a hook on the wall, he turned the lock and pushed. It opened into a garden, walled on both sides and bursting with leaves and buds: trees and ground were thick with greenery of every shade and tone. Succulents hugged the turf; taller stems held their petals proudly aloft, their heads waving gently in the breeze, reminding Heidi of the Munchkins.

'Come,' said Theo. 'Follow me to the summerhouse.'

The garden was longer than it first appeared. They walked through a thicket of trees until it opened into a large clearing with bird-trays and bird-baths. At the end was a stone building, circular and wide open at the front.

'Welcome to the heart of the Emerald City,' said the old man. 'I keep a few treasures here – mostly the birds, of course. They seem to like it here. But see,' he said as they followed him into the stone building, 'sit and be at peace.'

They sat on the bench that curved its way around the circular wall. The pictures Theo had painted the previous week were temporarily fixed around it. Nooks and crannies held statues of elephants and gods and snakes. In the center of the space was a table that held beautiful, large stones: Emeralds and other green treasures, some carved, some raw.

'What wonderful gems!' exclaimed Heidi. 'They seem to magnify the light of the evening sun.'

'I'd say this is more of a temple than a summerhouse,' said Greg.

'Perhaps so,' Theo agreed. 'It certainly stills my heart to sit here; makes it sing. And the heart is the gateway to the soul, I do believe.'

'And you told us last week,' said Greg, 'that the heart is a center of intelligence. Something like that, anyway. I'd love to know how that works.'

'Ah,' said the Professor. 'Maybe this is the very heart of the matter. There's a great force-field around that great pumping organ, you know.'

'No, I don't believe we did know,' said Dawn.

'Ah well, the energy-charge around the heart – or the power field – is a great deal larger than the one around the brain,' Theo continued. 'Five thousand times or so, to be precise. Get it into good working order, then, and that place sometimes known as the heart *center* will sort out anything you like, more or less. It will make your body stronger, for one thing, of course. Oh and it'll make everyone around you feel better. And it'll make *you* feel way better, of course: happier, calmer, richer, kinder.'

'And we get that force-field into good working order by doing what, exactly?' asked Frank.

'Various things,' replied Theo. 'Breathing good and deep; taking time to be still; making friends with yourself, with each other, with nature; being in the present. All of which means vanquishing the Wicked Witch, don't you know...'

'And finding the doorway that opens the way to the Wizard,' added Yasmin.

'Yes,' said Theo. 'And that in turn opens more doors, because the heart is the *connection*, you see. Through this wonderful force-field it has, it can connect us with all the forces of Creation. Now that's some resource. Get in touch with the power of a heart that's awake and you'll open doors to all the world; you'll get inspired. You can start creating all kinds of things.'

'Whole worlds, for instance,' said Heidi. 'Just like our friend in Oz.'

'Quite,' agreed Theo. 'Because you can have a pretty neat idea, let's say, a spark in your head that suggests you might like to transform living spaces, set up your own company or excel in martial arts. But it's the passion, the force of feeling, that really fuels the idea. It won't get off the ground until you fuel it.'

'Which has already happened,' said Yasmin, 'in some cases. Or nearly. Frank's in love – like properly in love – at last.'

Dawn blushed and took hold of a deep-green stone for closer examination.

'Thanks for the subtlety,' said Frank. 'It may even help my cause,' he added, catching Dawn's eye for a fraction of a second.

'You're welcome,' Yasmin replied. 'Greg's strumming leaves Bob Dylan in the shade. Joseph's grand designs get grander by the month – he could bring the Bronx back to life.'

'In the blink of an eye,' said the Professor. 'So you don't have to worry too much about those thoughts you wanted to cancel, Jo. As long as our downbeat thoughts don't carry too much charge, we can generally over-ride them when we turn the beam up. Heart-power, you see! I come out here when I wish to engage it – what a gift! But it can be done anywhere: on the bus, in the library...'

'That's a relief,' said Joseph. 'There's more than a few thoughts I could cancel out – three months' backlog at least.'

'Piece of cake,' said Theo. 'You'll do it in no time. There's genius in the making in all of you. You see this yellow road?' he said, pointing to one of the pictures on the wall. 'Look how it arrives at the base of that tree. And look how that beam of light comes straight down from somewhere Up There, right through the trunk, and deep into the ground.'

'And look how the yellow road intersects with it,' said Greg, taking a deep breath.

'Thank you,' said their teacher. 'And congratulations! When the path we tread, with all its hazards and bumps, is accepted, we stop fighting and resisting it; we bring it all back home: our story, the things we've done and seen. To be integrated and incorporated, of course. There's the crux of the matter, you see,' he said, putting his finger on the center of the crossroads between the yellow road and the vertical light beam. 'Right in the heart. It's the place where our experience crosses with our soul-beam. Informs it, even.'

Greg took a long, deep breath. 'You mean even our souls keep on learning?' he said.

'Oh yes,' replied Theo. 'We've forgotten so much, you see, in the thousands of years we've been getting ourselves stuck in those poppy fields down here – in a manner of speaking.'

'So you mean that once the heart wakes up, so to say, we can start reconnecting with our hidden power?' said Frank the scientist. 'What a wonderfully encouraging prospect! I hope it works.'

'No worries on that score,' said Theo. 'We're all doing that; we shall all reclaim our sovereignty one day, get re-established in our light. Some of us do it slower, some faster – but the outcome is assured. So when we give up resisting the tricky bits on our paths, and start understanding the reason why we put them there in the first place...'

'We really did that, did we?' said Joseph. 'I'm just checking there's no exceptions.'

'No exceptions,' said Theo, 'as far as I've ever discovered. And when we integrate the lessons of those tricky bits, when we stop sabotaging ourselves with our everlasting complaints and petty judgments of ourselves, of each other, of our life conditions, then our path brings us right back home, it intersects with that delicious beam of light – otherwise known as our divinity, our eternal self, or the part of us that's connected with love and power. *Divine* love and power, no less. Look at that wonderful beam: pretty, isn't it? I rather like that whiter shade of gold.'

'It's beautiful,' said Heidi.

'Of course it is,' said Theo. 'It's your connection with the Wizard, the hotline to your higher self. He planned it all the way along, remember? He, She, It – that rather more enlightened part of your awareness than you meet in the everyday run of things – knew precisely where you needed to go, and how to get there. The ego will tend to skirt around it, of course: it avoids the real power of presence like the plague. But the ego always runs out of steam in the end. Then the heart-door that shut so long ago eases its way open. Ah, the relief!'

'So you mean that when the road of our life gets hooked up with that beam,' said Heidi, 'dissolves into it, even, we're pretty much right on track.'

'Right on track,' agreed the Professor. 'Your time-limited ego merges with your big Self. And the big Self has no sell-by date, you see! It keeps on going – eternally, so far as I know. And since it pretty much wrote your script for you, it's always ahead of the game. Your ego is just its servant really: it's the scout; goes out and collects useful information.'

'Which it adds to the database,' suggested Frank.

'Right on,' said Theo. 'Information is power, after all. So self-information grows into Self-power. Or soul-power – it's the same thing.'

'So what's the formula?' asked Dawn. 'I can't wait! How do we set about this business of getting the thing you call the heart center up and running? What can we do this week that will kick-start the process?'

'Oh, you're doing it already,' replied Theo, 'excellent practitioners that you are. You can allow yourselves to feel a little more, perhaps – if you choose. Feeling things fully instead of suppressing them is always good.'

'And then you can let them go,' said Greg.

'Quite so,' said the Professor. 'No need to hang on to anything that's outlived its purpose. Take a little time out to breathe a little deeper, to bring in even more light than you're shining already. Think about what you'd like to give the world, maybe, to keep the flow going nicely. That's always a sensible thing to do.'

'Which means we need to start believing in what we have and are,' said Dawn, 'so that we have something useful to *give* away.'

'You're quite right,' said Theo. 'It's just as I say – working on ourselves, or getting to know ourselves if you like, amounts to enlightened self-interest, empowerment. So how about doing just one thing this week that makes you feel seriously good – without the "seriously", of course? All is one and one is all, you see, in the end. We're part of one another, however much it may feel like we're not. You can help the world no end by feeling good, you know.'

'I feel seriously good sitting right here in the Temple,' said Heidi.

'And as you live that feeling,' Theo replied, 'as you feel that way more and more often, you create your own power-centers wherever you go.'

'Thanks for the permission,' said Dawn. 'I feel freer already.'

'Excellent. The heart's the place that brings it all together, you see. It's the place where we all meet, so chances are that if you're feeling bad, you'll be helping someone else to feel the same way. But cultivate the spark, on the other hand, polish up your brilliance and your good cheer, and you can add it to the Universal pot. Then *everyone* cheers up. The more Godly sparks there are in there, the better.'

'That takes sharing to a whole new level,' said Frank.

'It does,' agreed the Professor. 'Along with the concept of accepting our rather tricky egos. We really have to develop and hone our special skills, you know; we have to become a someone, if you like. Then, when we're ready, we take the core of that well-rounded someone and give it all away.'

'Are you sure that's a good idea?' asked Joseph, a slightly nervous laugh hovering around his throat.

'Oh yes,' the old man replied. 'It's an excellent plan. We're a little like trees, I suppose: they take their seeds, or their ego-gifts if you like, and donate them to the earth. Makes more trees: everyone wins, you see: just look at this happy garden. You'll be doing the same with your buildings, after all – and would you say that you'll be losing anything by doing that?'

Joseph was silent for a few moments. 'Of course not,' he said suddenly. 'I understand that. It's the very opposite of losing something, of course it is.'

There was silence for a while as they thought about their teacher's words. Heidi walked over to one of his rough paintings and gazed at it a while.

'So what can *we* do for *you*?' she asked, turning to Theo.

'Oh you've no idea how much you do for me already,' the old man replied. 'Every time we meet, I learn something new. Can't tell you how wonderful that is. I shall be counting the days until I see you again,' he smiled.

'Hang on, though,' said Dawn. 'Before we go, there's still a bit of a question. Dorothy opened the door to her heart. She worked pretty hard to ease it open, so to speak, a crack at least, but then she had to leave it again, poor kid. Why wasn't she allowed in, *really*? I mean you said she'd got even *more* work to do, but you'd think that staying in the heart center – if that's the Emerald City – would be the fast route to everything she's trying to achieve, if it's all it's cracked up to be.'

'Ah,' said Theo, 'but no-one is really shutting her out except herself. Tough, isn't it – we find the perfect living conditions, run the marathon, get the promotion, and we think our lives are all tickety-boo at last – and it's *still* not enough. Our pesky *small* selves throw up a whole new set of problems to deal with. That's the bad news…'

'But maybe Dorothy's only just getting a handle on her power,' suggested Greg.

'Exactly,' said their teacher. 'That's the crux of the matter. You turn up the beam, your ego screams and has a fling – or someone else's does. It just means there's more needs looking at – more dark corners to clear out. Itchy doubts and fears, that kind of thing, pulling us back so we can love them into safety. That clears them right out of the way, so we can move into radical trust. And *there's* the good news: a chance for a big life-change, if ever there was one.'

'So the Wizard's doing her a favor, banishing her,' said Frank. 'He's pushing her to do the thing thoroughly, to catch sight of the murky bits while the lights are on.'

'That's why the Wicked Witch brings on the flying monkeys, then,' said Yasmin. 'Her major power-tool, her last-ditch resort. They're pretty nifty, too: they can lift you right up and dump you in that ferocious castle of hers. Which they do, of course.'

'Dorothy will have to tackle the crone face to face, then,' said Theo.

'Yes,' said Heidi, 'but she's already glimpsed the Emerald City. She knows what she's aiming for. She's seen and felt just enough of it to spur her on.'

'She has,' agreed Theo. 'And it's a funny thing about fears: when we look at them head-on, in the full light of day so to speak, or open our hearts to them, even, then we find that they really have very little power. They're just like everything else – longing to be loved. All it takes is a little bucket of water to wash them clean away! Or transform them into something friendly.'

'Well, Apollo,' said Heidi, 'you sure make it look easy, in a paradise like this.'

'It's easier than we think,' the old man replied. He yawned. 'But it's been a long day. I shall turn in now. Have a wonderful week,' he said, as he rose to make his way back through the garden, 'now the days are warming up. It has to be seven seriously good days, remember?'

They walked until they reached the more familiar door at the other end of the house.

'If you'll be kind enough to come and visit an old man again next week,' Theo said as he waved them off, 'we'll go back with Dorothy to that Emerald City. We'll see if our friend the Wizard will let her into the Inner Temple – for real.'

Over the Rainbow

'Well, well,' Theo greeted his young friends as they trooped into the familiar kitchen for the final chapter of the module they had enjoyed so much. 'Back so soon. Have you destroyed the Wicked Witch already? You know what this means? It is time to go home. I shall have to start handing out medals and all sorts, ready for the homeward trip.'

'It's not!' said Heidi emphatically. 'We *are* home anyway – we only just got here.'

'And that's just where the old duffer told Dorothy to be, right at the start,' the teacher replied. 'You're good students all.'

'She meant home is where *you* are, Grandpa,' said Greg, as they filled vases with fresh-scented freesias and roses.

'And that's just where she's wrong,' the Professor replied, gazing warmly at Heidi. 'What beautiful blooms, you dear people! Thank you. But look, there's a thing, right outside the window, after these refreshing showers. Showing Heidi that she's quite right – she's home already.'

'It's a perfect rainbow!' said Yasmin with delight.

'It's so thick and lush,' said Joseph, 'you'd think the angels just took out their paintbrushes.'

'Maybe they did,' said Theo. 'Or maybe they just beamed an extra dose of light through the clouds. *More* light. It's a funny thing about light – it never abandons us – and it has no limits. It feeds us, educates, keeps us warm; it even takes us home.'

'Rainbows?' said Heidi. 'And that's supposed to mean we're home already?'

'Of course,' Theo replied. 'Just like Noah after that dreadful flood; or Dorothy after all those scary things that happened to her. Whip out the paintbrush, or beam a little light – they're home in no time. Just like us.'

'I'm not sure I get it,' said Frank.

'Oh but you will,' replied the teacher cheerfully. 'How goes the story? Our young heroine's story, that is: I'm sure you all have plenty of your own.'

'Those last few tasks are quite a thing for Dorothy – and all of them,' said Heidi, 'before they're allowed back in to anything even remotely "homeish". It's all about going to the extremities, just like you said. The poor old Scarecrow gets all the stuffing knocked out of him and he's left for dead. Dorothy has to destroy the miserable hag once and for all.'

'Which means a ride with those flying monkeys,' said Yasmin. 'Cool!'

'So she goes right into the wicked creature's castle, doesn't she?' asked Theo. 'Right into the dark. Once she's been cut off from her unfortunate friends...'

'Until Toto escapes and runs off to rescue them,' said Dawn.

'Of course,' said Theo. 'Toto will never let his friend down, not in a million years.'

'Then they all come to join her,' said Frank, 'and accidentally splash water on the old hag, just as you mentioned last week. It sees her off completely.'

'Excellent,' said Theo. 'Clear pure water; clear pure light. Great cleansers.'

'So they get another ride,' added Yasmin. 'Those deadly monkeys turn into their best mates, take them right to the Wizard's front door. For free.'

'Ah well,' remarked Theo. 'That does tend to happen, you know. The very worst things we have to face can turn into life's greatest blessings, when only we dare to flip the coin. Just wait a year or two and you will no doubt find the same.'

'Oh, we did that already,' said Joseph. 'With a little help from our friends. Made a start, anyway.'

'Good work,' replied Theo. 'Does that also mean you did something this week that made you feel seriously good?'

'I accepted an invitation from Yasmin,' Joseph grinned, 'to go meet one of the new kids she's coaching. Her star pupil – and I'm not surprised...'

'They got on like a house on fire,' said Yasmin, 'so I left them to it.'

'And I hope that made you feel seriously great as well!' laughed their teacher, addressing the ever-cheerful Yasmin.

'Sure,' she replied. 'I don't offer guarantees, mind – I just do the intros.'

'So how about events in Oz?' Theo asked. 'Does the old duffer in the heart of the land give our friends a warm reception this time?'

'Pretty much,' said Heidi. 'But they have to get through some nonsense first. It's Toto who shows Dorothy the truth, of course. The old trumpet is blaring – the smoke and mirrors stuff; blown-up faces near the ceiling and all that – until Toto scampers off and grabs a curtain. *Whoosh!* There's the little man behind the screen, chatting away into a loudspeaker, pretending to be a know-all Wizard. Rubbish, all of it. Dorothy's mad at him. Who wouldn't be?'

'Always hard,' sighed Theo, 'having our illusions shattered. And so empowering. It should happen to every one of us on a regular basis. Keeps us awake.'

'She tells him he's all wrong,' added Dawn, 'a rotten, bad man. He disagrees, of course, about being a bad man, but admits he's a lousy Wizard. But then out come the medals and testimonials and all the rest of it. Telling them they're perfect just as they are, and always have been and always will be, more or less. You know, the Scarecrow's been a bright spark, the Tin Woodman's been full of love; even the Lion's found he can be brave when he's put to the test.'

'Maybe no-one took the trouble to point any of that out to them before,' suggested Greg. 'I don't remember anyone back home ever suggesting I was whole, or perfect or anything, when I was a kid.'

'Or since,' said Heidi. 'Except you,' she added, speaking to Theo.

'It's a handy thing when someone points this out to us frail human beings,' agreed Theo, 'as we're always feeling so incomplete. Our quirky bunch of friends has made quite some discovery of this innate perfection already, of course, on their trek along the Yellow Brick Road.'

'While they were so absorbed in present-moment living they couldn't really *not* discover all those gifts and strengths they'd been blessed with,' commented Heidi.

'Indeed,' said the Professor. 'The power of now: it's really unlimited, you know.'

Folding his hands in his lap happily, and closing his eyes, their teacher took a long, deep breath. Everyone was silent. Joseph noticed suddenly, and with some surprise, that he was feeling perfectly happy, perfectly at peace.

'So it really will soon be time for Dorothy to go home,' Theo continued after a while, 'if she has uncovered her latent magnificence.'

'And the Wizard of Oz or whoever he is – Professor Marvel perhaps – agrees to take her back with him in his balloon,' said Heidi, 'but then he leaves without her. Believe me, I remember that feeling...'

'Ah, I know you do,' said Theo warmly. 'But how's your week been, Heidi? Did you find something to make you feel...'

'*Seriously* good!' she exclaimed. 'I wrote the first three pages of my movie script. Oh and...' she added with a quiet smile, 'I decided to hang in with Greg: I'm about to venture up North instead of retreating back East.'

'And *my* seriously brilliant piece of work this week was in persuading her to come,' added Greg. 'I hope you've got some medals for me – I sure deserve them.'

'Perfect,' smiled Theo. 'Glinda must have come to call. There's nothing like the power of love. We all need reminding of who we *really* are – and more often than you may think. Once we get a handle on that, the direction falls into place in no time. Look at how it goes for Dorothy: a few clicks of her heels, one, two, three! – full power of the Trinity, right there inside her, and then... Oh, but she must say goodbye to her beloved friends first, mustn't she? She must embrace them, acknowledge them, integrate them: her cleverness, her courage and love – and everything, all of it. And after that...'

'It's over the rainbow,' said Greg. 'Right back home.'

'Perfect plan,' said their teacher. 'And you know what God himself said to that hairy Neanderthal Noah, after that famous washout? He showed him the "bow" in the sky, said it would be there forever.'

'As an eternal covenant,' added Greg.

'Oh yes,' agreed Theo. 'It was a promise, most certainly – and we have to take promises very seriously.'

'So what was "God" promising, exactly?' asked Frank.

'That he wouldn't let you forget the heart of the matter, the thing that lights you up and makes it all worthwhile, whatever the "it" might be in your case or mine. He was promising an eternal bridge back home: now that's some promise indeed.'

'That would be it, then,' said Frank. 'That would be why I felt majorly wonderful after I'd spent three days alone this week right up in the hills, looking at how I've done life like a bull in a china shop, without too much stopping to think. I've been finding out quite a few things – like what I really want, for instance.'

'Which is?' asked Theo.

'To feel safe enough to dive in deep,' Frank replied. 'Just like you said. Commitment: that's what I really, truly want.'

'Oh my giddy aunt,' said Yasmin, grinning from ear to ear as she looked from Frank to Dawn and back again. 'Do you deserve a medal or what?'

'A testimonial, please,' Frank replied. 'I may be needing one.'

'I guess that's what happens,' said Heidi, 'when you shine light into the darkness – any darkness. It kind of reminds it of the other part of itself. We find it when we get away from our run-of-the-mill doings and take some time out for a bit of soul-searching.'

'It's exactly what happens,' said Theo. 'Shine a light into a dark place and what do you find arises at the very place where they meet? A rainbow! Shine the light of who we really are, then, behind all those little myths held dear by our poor, deluded egos, with all their stress and confusion, into the rich, fertile layers of darkness inside our selves, and what do we get?'

'Another rainbow,' said Heidi. 'The personal kind. It's just like my dad told me, once in a lullaby – so to say. He used to show me the rainbows in the sky and tell me they were wonderful bridges. He must have meant a whole lot more than I understood back then. He must have been saying they take us from our impotent, ignorant selves into our powerful ones.'

'Yes,' agreed Theo, 'and our loving ones. Which is the same thing, of course.'

'The rainbows are not necessarily the kind we can see, mind,' added Heidi. 'It's more of a feeling, knowing thing, I guess.'

'Where you feel and know the different parts of yourself,' agreed Theo. 'A path where all the multi-colored horses inside you can trot and meet and merge, and above all understand one another.'

'So what's the point of it?' asked Frank. 'What's the point of all the stress and hassle on the journey, if we knew all that we needed to know before we left home, in a manner of speaking? Why do we have to lose touch with all that wisdom and love and sheer common sense, just to come here and mess up?'

'Oh but we didn't know it all,' Theo replied. 'We're learning and learning, all the time – remember? The ego is out there doing some very useful scouting about. And you know very well that we don't come here and *only* mess up. Besides, the discovery of what you are *not* is an excellent route to finding what you are, you know. How could all that beautiful light and truth, and all the delightfulness that is the stuff of undiluted love, possibly see how wonderful it is without a bit of contrast here and there?'

'It's just as I thought,' added Yasmin. 'Without the help of the crone, we'd hardly know we were born.'

'And if we never felt like orphans, we'd never dig deep for all those hidden treasures,' said Theo. 'And we'd miss out on an awful lot of fun,' he added. 'Wasn't it on that very yellow road itself that they found the joy in navigating life at all, after all? They got well stuck into the moment. No past regrets, no future anxieties – full presence. That's something indeed. It's what happens when we enter the story with all our hearts.'

'The story that we wrote for ourselves,' added Heidi. 'That's what you told us: we write our own life-scripts.'

'Just so,' said the Professor, 'to entertain ourselves. There's no better vehicle for learning, after all, than a good story. Of course we get wrapped up in the drama,' he continued, 'the soap opera – so naturally we quite forget that we wrote the thing ourselves. But the Wizard never forgets. He's your higher self; he's there all the time, quietly running the show – from behind the screen. Oh and by the way, he loves you, from start to finish – and beyond, of course.'

'That's a good thought,' said Dawn. 'Makes me feel warm all over.'

'Isn't it just?' Theo agreed. 'So how about you, Dawn? How's your story going? What kind of seriously present-moment delights did you discover this week?'

'Oh I went to the gym!' she laughed. 'Been spending way too much time stuck up in my head. I figured my body needed attention.'

'Good on you,' said Yasmin. 'And how are *you* doing on the commitment front?' she grinned.

'Steady on!' Dawn replied. 'I've done my seriously good

assignment for *one* week.'

'The Wizard would be proud of you,' said Theo warmly. 'All of you. Good work, gathering up your resources – the bits of you that you'd forgotten or given away – and bringing them all back home.'

'Does Dorothy really have to go back to the grey zone?' Heidi asked. 'It seems a tough thing to ask of her after all the work she's done. Back to the Kansas prairies, the monochrome trees, the swine...'

'Oh no,' replied Theo with enthusiasm. 'We can't really get away from the light, however hard we may try. It makes us, after all; it sustains us; it even sends messages to us. The cells of our bodies chat to one another using the messages of light. Even the planets do it – hey Greg!'

'OK,' Greg replied. 'I'll remember to tell that to my dad.'

'But Dorothy has nothing to worry about, back in the grey zone,' the Professor continued. 'The light's been turned on inside her. Her family is convinced that she has lost her mind. What they don't realize is she's actually just found it – for the first time. She'll probably paint the town red, in a manner of speaking.'

'Maybe she just has to remember that rainbow bridge,' said Heidi.

'Exactly,' said Theo. 'Once in place, always in place. Young Dorothy is in touch with the powers of the Universe itself: lighting up the old prairies will be a walk in the park. And for you too, of course,' he added. 'The Kingdom of G-O-D is within you, remember – that's what we've all been told. All we have to do is believe it, and make it true within us.'

The rainbow was fading, along with the evening light. Their teacher was beginning to yawn.

'I shall turn in early tonight,' he said. 'You enjoy yourselves; stay as long as you please. Help yourselves to coffee, biscuits, cheese, beer, you know where it all lives. There's piles of paper and pens on the side; dream-catchers, wishing bowls, magic flutes, whatever you like. Make your scripts, or remake them; build your grandest visions – go ahead. The sky's not the limit, you know! Far from it.'

'So they were wrong on that, too, were they?' laughed Heidi. 'Whoever *they* are?'

'Quite wrong,' he agreed. 'And you're a dream team,' he added, 'just like the one that Dorothy built for herself. Now that is a first-class preparation for any project, large or small. Good night, my dears, good friendships, and good cheer.'

Heidi felt a pang of sadness as her beloved teacher stood up to leave. He looked at her and smiled, a deep, warm glow lighting up his wrinkled face. Greg squeezed Heidi's hand before he crossed the room and gave the old man a hug. The group of friends sat around the table for a time, a gentle silence filling the room.

'I gotta go,' said Yasmin a few moments later. 'I'm off early in the morning. Come fly with me,' she sighed dramatically, 'someone, anyone! Or I shall have to do it all alone.'

'Some chance!' grinned Joseph. 'Have a great time, though. Speaking for myself, I'm fully taken up this weekend, well, some of it at least. In fact I'm meeting her in half an hour. Let's walk that way together.'

'I must be off too,' said Frank. 'The end of the dissertation calls. But there's time for a short visit on the way – Bamboo Lounge for a fill-up. How about you,' he said, looking across at Dawn. 'Click your heels three times and we'll be there...' He bent down on one knee and brandished a borrowed freesia below her nose. 'Any hope?'

'Maybe you'll need to click your heels together too,' she replied. 'And yes, I'm coming.'

'Bye!' they called as they all left. 'Have a good weekend.' The old man was gone already, quietly vanished down the corridor.

Heidi looked around the peaceful room. 'I don't want to leave just yet,' she said. 'This is one class I really don't want to finish.'

'You don't have to leave,' said Greg. 'And maybe, you know, the class is just beginning.'

He sat at the piano, quietly improvising. *Greg could make music out of a tin can,* Heidi figured, as the gentle harmonies slid like warm silk, right through her veins.

She fingered the random assortment of pens, brushes, prayer mats; the rulers, stories, pictures and song sheets that overflowed from the old man's dresser untidily, abundantly, adding somehow to the peacefulness of the place. Taking hold of a pen and paper in one hand, a dream-catcher in the other, she sat down at the table and doodled for a while on the pad.

'I've got it,' she said. 'I have to really let rip with that movie script. I don't care if no-one ever reads it – it's bursting to come out. Those starter pages the other day – they did something, like turning on a tap.'

'Or stepping onto the Yellow Brick Road,' Greg smiled. 'Well,' he added, 'there's no time like the present. And no place, of course, like...'

'Yeah OK,' she said, as the new rush of words started to arrive.

Then she paused for a moment, looking over at him.

'Home,' she said. 'It's true; it's properly true. Home *is* in the pen – or the notes on the keyboard, or the feeling as you sit and watch the surf. I know it; I really know it. But when I go visit my family in Boston, you'll come too, right?'

'Right,' he agreed.

The notes wafted over from the piano as Heidi's words tumbled on to the page, and then the sounds gently faded into silence. They both gazed gratefully, a little wistfully, towards the long corridor, towards the rooms that held the old teacher's own story in their walls as he slept. Closing the door softly behind them, they walked out into the silvery light of a rising moon.

*

Author Note

Stories are not only the best medium humanity has devised for learning and relaxation; they are the stuff of our own lives, of course, as well. The events of our lives, and the stories we tell ourselves about them, may raise us up, they may educate us, but some of those stories – if we allow them to do so – will also run us, and not in a good way.

So when, a few years ago, I received a message, or a directive from some kind of other dimension, to 'remove the story from the body energetically' I understood what kinds of stories were being talked about: the ones built in Kansas, so to say, rather than Oz; the ones built from our fears and traumatic experiences, rather than those constructed from joy. This simple message turned out to be the beginning of the life-transforming Metatronic Healing™ system, which is being widely taken up by medics and lawyers, aid workers and healers of all kinds. As old 'stories' – the limiting versions of reality that so many of us tend to keep repeating – are dissolved, this makes space for something new. A much higher frequency of light enters the system, bringing with it all manner of gifts which are life-changing.

If you're looking for something you've not quite found yet, if you're coping with low energy, dis-ease, depression or any of the countless discomforts that beset us on planet earth, or if you are a therapist wishing to expand your toolkit, do visit us at the website below. You will find general information, classes, practitioners, online downloads and more.

I'd like to thank a few people before I finish: John Hunt of O Books, along with Trevor Greenfield and Catherine Harris, are a dream team for anyone aspiring to put their ramblings into print. Thank you for all your help in this and my previous book, *Rescued by Angels*. Thank you, Lisa O'Connell, for sharp-eyed and generous early edits; and Carol Nayach, Nikki Shabbo and Clare Glennon, for well-timed encouragement: sunlight and water to any book, especially on slow days. Thank you, John, beloved husband, for making all of this work possible: Metatronic Healing™ which we know to be useful, and this book which we hope will be. Above all, in relation to *this* book, I send a vast and awed thanks to my children, Nicola, Stephen and Magdalen: I couldn't have done a single step of my journey through *Kansas* or *Oz* without you. You are the best friends that any girl could ever hope to find.

Please come and visit us at www.metatronic-life.com

BOOKS

O is a symbol of the world, of oneness and unity. In different cultures it also means the "eye," symbolizing knowledge and insight. We aim to publish books that are accessible, constructive and that challenge accepted opinion, both that of academia and the "moral majority."

Our books are available in all good English language bookstores worldwide. If you don't see the book on the shelves ask the bookstore to order it for you, quoting the ISBN number and title. Alternatively you can order online (all major online retail sites carry our titles) or contact the distributor in the relevant country, listed on the copyright page.

See our website www.o-books.net for a full list of over 500 titles, growing by 100 a year.

And tune in to myspiritradio.com for our book review radio show, hosted by June-Elleni Laine, where you can listen to the authors discussing their books.

MySpiritRadio